# PRETTY B*TCHES GET EVEN

## BY

## T. FRIDAY

# Dedication

This book is dedicated to my five babies: Jordin Friday, Jacob Friday, Jacory Blount, Jakayla Blount, and Jalisa Blount. Just know that everything I do and every struggle I go through is so you guys don't have to worry about shit. I Love y'all.

# Acknowledgements

To my best friend Blunt, you have been in my corner every step of the way, and I love and appreciate you for that. You have tolerated me bugging you every day for the last 14 years and never gave up on me. We have a bond that nobody can break.

To the world's best publisher Racquel Williams, you rock! People always say make your first choice your best choice, and I truly believe that signing my very first book contract with you was the best thing that I could have done. I appreciate you giving me the opportunity to write for your dope company. I also appreciate how you push me to stay on top and to keep going no matter what.

To my pen sister Christine Davis, I owe you so much, lol. I swear your grind and dedication was all the motivation I needed to push my writing career. Much love to your sis.

To all my pen sisters and brothers in the urban industry, let's continue to use our imaginations and entertain the world, one book at a time.

To my wonderful readers and supporters, I just really want to say thank you from the bottom of my heart. You guys are awesome, and I appreciate you all for giving a new author a chance and still rocking 19 books later. I'm so happy to be some of you guys' favorite author. You all make me keep going strong.

To my baby sister, Amanda Jordin Hollis, there's not a day that you don't cross my mind. I swear 15 years wasn't long enough to have you here on earth with us. Love you so much my Lil' White Chick.
To my mom and dad, I wish you guys were here to see me doing something that I love. Continue to watch over me and the rest of our family.

# Chapter 1

"Darron, Darron get up!" 10-year-old Ayanna yelled as she tried to wake her older brother.

15-year-old Darron rolled over annoyed. "Man, what the fuck? What's up Yaya?" He asked, still half sleep.

"I'm hungry and ain't nothing in there to eat."

"Fuck! Where mama at?"

Yaya rolled her eyes. "She not here, boy, maybe she went to work. Now get up and find me something to eat."

As annoying she could be at times, Darron adored his baby sister and would do anything for her. He sat up knowing that if he didn't get up, she wasn't gonna let him go back to sleep. Finally climbing out of the bed, Darron went into the living room to turn the TV on for Yaya before going to check out what was in the kitchen.

"Find you some cartoons or something to watch while I go find you something to eat."

Their mother, Betty, was a single mom raising of them both on her own. Some luck she had to give a deadbeat muthafucka a second chance just to have him stick around long enough to get her pregnant for the second time. At times, things had gotten hard and her bills stacked higher than the paychecks she brought home. However, she tried her best to do for her kids.

Darron opened the fridge and didn't see shit in there but a few onions, a stick of butter and a box of baking soda. It wasn't until he walked over towards the counter that he saw a letter his mom wrote explaining that she was gonna go to the market once she got off work later that day. She also left $1 so that he could go get them some noodles to hold them over. Darren tossed the letter into the trash before tucking the dollar bill into his pocket. He then walked back into the living room.

"Aye, Yaya, I'm about to go Eddie's and get something for you. Mama's going to the market once she gets off work."

"You can't leave me here by myself, Darron, I wanna go," she whined, jumping up from the couch.

Darron shook his head. He didn't wanna take her 'cause she was only gonna slow him down and beg for everything in the store. With only a dollar in his pocket, he didn't wanna disappoint her.

"Look, Yaya, I'm only gonna be gone for a hot minute. I'm going right up the street to Eddie's store. You a big girl, you can hold it down here, can't you?"

"You right, I am a big girl. Plus, I remember what you told me."

Darron was puzzled. "What's that, Yaya?"

"You told me to never open the door for nobody and that you will always have your keys on you. You said to keep watching TV like I don't hear anything."

"That's right."

After getting dressed, Darron made his way towards Eddie's Liquor Store. It really was just up the street on the corner from their house, just like he had told Yaya.

"What's up, D?"

Darron looked up to see his homeboy, Marcus, standing outside of the store.

"What's up, nigga?"

"Nothing much, out here trying to make a few dollars. You know the early bird catches the worm."

Darron couldn't help but to laugh at his friend. His ass had always been a square type nigga, so it was hard to believe that he was out hitting the blocks.

"What's so funny, bro?" Marcus asked.

"I just never pictured you out here, that's it. Never thought you were that type," Darron explained.

"Man, it's hard out here and I need to be getting paid. If you were smart, you'll try to get down with me. We could be making money together, bro."

Darron knew his mom would kill him twice if she even thought that he was out here in these streets, but watching Marcus serve up a fiend and holding that small knot of money, he became curious.

Once the fiend walked away, Darron started asking questions. "So, who you working for, nigga?"

"I'm selling for that cockeyed nigga Sticks. You might have seen his ass around the way on these streets."

"Yeah, I know exactly who you talking about. How that shit happen, bro?"

"You know that nigga works for the big boss man Jackson. Well, he saw me one day and asked if I wanted to make a few extra dollars. Next thing you know, I was dropping off work to people. I did that for a few weeks before I learned the game and started working this corner. Where the fuck you been, bro? I've been getting money all summer."

"Damn, bro, for real? I've been in the house chilling with Yaya while my moms be at work."

"Nigga, it's time for you to jump off the porch and get your feet wet. Mama Betty has been working too hard by herself. When you gon' lift that load off her shoulders?"

Darron shook his head in agreement and after a few seconds of thinking over everything, he had made up his mind. "You're right, bro, so what's up? It's not gonna be a problem with you just pulling me in?"

"Hell nah, bro. Besides, he been told me to get someone to help me out. Look, I'm gonna be up here for a while, but tonight I gotta make a couple of rounds to drop some shit off. I'll pick you up and show you the ropes. We can split the bread afterwards."

Darron smiled. "Alright, nigga, I'm down."

Marcus walked away to serve the packet that he stashed in his pocket while Darron walked into the store.

Eddie watched Darron and most of the neighborhood kids grow up, so when Darron asked for a few things on credit, he didn't mind looking out for him. Darron grabbed the noodles, a loaf of bread and a pack of lunchmeat.

"That's it?" Eddie asked.

"Yeah, man, but I got a dollar to go towards my bill," Darron said, pulling out the dollar that his mom had left for him.

"No, no, no, you keep that and go get your sister some chips and a juice."

"You sure, Eddie?"

"Yeah, y'all some good kids, just don't get caught up in the street shit your friend out there on. I notice everything that goes on, but since I know his grandma, I haven't bothered to call the police on his stupid self yet. Anyways, go ahead and get her stuff, you're holding up my line."

Darron laughed as he looked around. No one else was in the store with him but Eddie. Darron walked away to get his sister chips and juice all while thinking about what Eddie said about Marcus. He wanted to be a man and help take care of his sister, but if he was gonna be out in these streets, he needed to make sure his mom never found out about what he was up to.

"Thanks again, Eddie."

"No problem, Darron," Eddie said as he turned to play an older guy's lottery.

Grabbing the bags from off the counter, Darron walked away with a warm heart knowing that there were still people out there to help him out. Marcus was walking back towards the store when Darron walked out of the store carrying his bags.

"Aye, I need to get back to the crib to Yaya but come by later."

"Alright, nigga, I got you."

Darron had already spent too much time out and away from the house, so he picked up his pace to make it back home to his baby sister.

~

"Darron, Darron!" Betty yelled out as she walked into the house.

After working on her feet for seven long straight hours and then walking around the super market, Betty was dead tired. Yaya was knocked out on the couch and after hearing his name being called, Darron ran into the living room.

"Hey, ma," he said, grabbing the bags from out her hand.

"Hey, it's some more bags in the trunk. Go get them for me," she ordered.

"Alright, I got you. Have a seat and relax, ma."

Betty smiled as she walked over towards the couch. She loved how helpful her son was around the house. Although his father wasn't around and she had been holding things down on her own, she knew that she had him on the right track. When she heard women around the way talking about their teenage sons in the streets doing dumb shit that could get them locked up or even get them killed, she felt good knowing that it wasn't her son in the middle of that bullshit.

Later that evening, just as promised, Marcus came by the house to pick Darron up. He knocked on the screen door twice before Betty came to the door.

"Hey, Ms. Fisher, how are you doing?" He asked, walking in the front room.

"I'm doing great boy. I swear your ass gets taller every time I see you. How's your grandma doing around there?"

"She's doing good, ma'am."

"That's good to hear. My job got me working on Sunday mornings now, so I haven't been able to see her at church. Once they hire someone else, I'm gonna request at least two Sundays off a month so I can get back into the church."

Marcus wasn't really trying to hear all that church talk, but he smiled as if he cared.

"That's cool, I'll let her know."

Betty walked out the room and into her son's room. As she peeked into the room, she could see that he was reading a book about those race cars that he loved.

"Hey, Marcus is out there for you. What are y'all about to get into?"

"Nothing really. We ain't seen each other that much, so we're about to just walk around and play catch up."

In Betty's eyes, Marcus was a good boy, unlike his older brothers, so she trusted Darron to hang around him. "Ok, just be back at a decent time. I'm about to take my ass to bed. I'm tired and got to get up in the morning."

"Ok, ma, I'll be right back."

Betty sat on her bed lost in her thoughts. She was tired but knew that she wouldn't be able to sleep until her son returned to the house safe and in one piece.

Darron walked out to the front room and saw Marcus sitting on the couch waiting for him. "What's up, you ready?"

"Yeah, come on," Darron answered.

Darron walked out of his mama's house knowing that what he was about to get into would kill her. As long as he handled his business, didn't get caught and brought home a few bucks, he could at least buy some food to help out.

"So, run this shit by me again. What I gotta do to make this bread again?"

As they walked up the street, Marcus explained everything to him once again. "Listen, we're gonna go meet up with that nigga Sticks at his spot…."

Before he could finish, Darron cut him off. "Wait a minute, we're gonna be working in the spot?" He asked.

"Hell nah, nigga. Let me finish telling you the plan. After we meet up at the spot, he's gonna give me the work and let me know who get what. We make the couple of runs then we come back here to get paid. Now since you helping me out, I'll be the one to pay you. Do you understand that shit now?"

"Yeah, bro, I get it," he answered.

Darron had taken in all the information that was given to him. Everything sounded simple as hell, but he was still a little nervous. He had watched those hood movies and even listened to music with niggas rapping about that hood life. He knew for sure that he wasn't about that lifestyle. As much as he wanted to turn around and go back home, he kept walking. He didn't want his friend to think that he was a scary pussy.

The guys had walked a few more blocks before stopping in front of what looked like a vacant house.

"Wait out here and let me go holler at Sticks," Marcus said before walking towards the back of the house.

Darron stood outside for what seemed twenty whole minutes, waiting on Marcus to walk back around front. "See, nigga, this God's way of giving you a chance to just walk away before shit gets too real," Darron mumbled to himself.

Just as he had decided to walk home, Marcus called out to him. "Aye, bro, where your ass going?"

"Man, you was taking too long, I was headed for the crib."

Marcus laughed. "You crazy as hell, bro. Anyways, that nigga Sticks be on some bullshit sometimes. He was supposed to have my shit bagged up and ready for me. Instead, he was in that bitch getting head from that cracked bitch that be at the gas station begging for change all the fucking time. Then that nigga made me wait for them to be done. After that, he was supposed to get my bag together, but he couldn't even stay woke. That muthafucka was in there nodding off and shit. If I didn't know any better, I'd say that nigga was getting high off Jackson's work."

"Damn, nigga, for real? Jackson ain't the one to fuck with. If he knew about that fool getting high, he'll kill that nigga."

"Hell yeah, but that's the thing. If Jackson finds out then Sticks is gonna be out of a damn job, which means we gonna be out of a job. The way I'm looking at shit, as long as the work and money straight, then we good," Marcus explained.

"Yeah, you're right," was all that Darron could say.

They made their way up the bock to start their journey. Everything went smooth and exactly two and a half hours later, they were returning to the spot that they had went to earlier.

"Let me get this money from this nigga. Wait right here and don't be trying to sneak off, bro," Marcus ordered.

Darron chuckled. "I'm not, just hurry up."

Ten minutes had passed and Marcus came out shaking his head again at what he witnessed.

"Yeah, that nigga getting high."

"You saw him do the shit?"

"Hell yeah. That nigga did two lines in my face before handing over the money. I guess that's how we know he still at the beginning of his drug habit. A real fiend ain't giving up any money. And that bitch still up in there with him."

"That nigga got AIDS!" Darron yelled out, laughing,

They both laughed as they continued to head toward their block.

"Man, on some real shit, I really appreciate you coming out and helping me tonight. I know that this shit is not even how you really get down. That shit be easy money, but I hate being out here by myself."

Marcus then dug down in his pocket. Pulling out a few bills, he handed over $200. "This all you, bro."

"Good looking, bro."

That night, Darren wondered exactly how much he could make if he had his own route. He wasn't trying to be greedy, but what he did that night was simple and an easy $200. He could make double that running his own route. He was jumping the gun in his head, but his thoughts were everywhere. He even thought that if he saved right, he could probably move them away. Everything sounded good until he thought about where he was gonna tell his mama the money came from.

For the next week, Darren had been leaving Yaya at home by herself while his mom was at work. He made sure Yaya ate breakfast and knew not to open the door for anyone. He spent his days on the block with Marcus and later in the evening, he was making runs. He made sure they ate good, but other than that, he stacked all the bread that he made with Marcus. The job wasn't hard, and he was able to catch on quick.

"Shit slow motion out here, bro. I'm about to go to the crib to check on Yaya's ass."

"Ok, cool, bro. I'm gonna holler at you later."

Before heading home, he went to the market to grab a few groceries for the house. He knew they were getting low on food and it was gonna be a few days before his mom got paid again.

Betty walk in the door later that night tired as hell. Since they had let go one of the cashiers at the Coney Island where she worked, Betty had been working extra hard as a cashier and waitress most days.

"What's that smell?" She hollered, walking towards the kitchen.

Yaya jumped up from the dinner table then ran to give her mom a hug. "Hi, Mama! Darren's making us a special dinner," she said, full of excitement.

Betty walked over towards her son. She quickly slapped him up the side of his head and started to yell. "Boy, I know like hell you ain't out here in these streets!" "Dang, ma, what the hell you hit me for?" Darron asked, holding his head.

"Boy, you better watch your mouth when you're talking to me. How did you get the money for this food, Darron?

Darren knew this day was coming and still didn't have a story together. Because he didn't have time to really think things through, he quickly blurted out the first thing that came to mind, praying that he didn't get hit again.

"Ma, I didn't say nothing because I knew you don't like for Yaya being here by herself, but I got a job at the car wash to help out around here."

"Doing what, Darron?"

"I help out drying a few cars, then I come home to make sure Yaya good. I make sure she gets something to eat for lunch, then I leave for a few more hours before I come back home. Everything's working out, ma."

Betty took a seat at the table next to Yaya. She felt bad for hitting him and he was just trying to help her out. Her baby boy was becoming a young man and trying to pick up the slack that their dad had left.

"I'm sorry for overreacting, Darron. It's just that you're at the age where you could easily be influenced into doing dumb shit. And when I saw all this food in here cooking, I just knew that you had made the decision to run these streets for some easy money."

Darron turned his head to look at the food that was almost done. He couldn't believe how he just sat in his mom's face and lied about what he had been up to. He felt guilty, but at the same time, he was loving the feeling of having money in his pocket.

"Ma, let's just drop the subject and eat dinner."

Betty didn't bring the situation back up. She smiled watching her son serve them some fried chicken, baked Mac and Cheese, greens, yams and cornbread.

"Ma, don't look like that. You know you taught us how to throw down in this kitchen."

"I sure did," she replied.

Yaya yelled out, "I helped too, Mommy!"

"I bet you did, baby girl, and I know that it's gonna be the best meal ever."

# Chapter 2

Darron and Marcus walked out of Stick's spot holding the envelop that contained their payment. Soon as they hit the front of the house, they opened it up and instantly got pissed.

"Man, that nigga tripping. How the fuck does he think $300 is gonna be enough for the both of us?" Marcus said, looking at the bills.

"Fuck you mean it's only $300? Yeah, that nigga got us fucked up. We make more than that shit a piece on a good day," Darron said, feeling played.

"Bro, I know, so what now?"

Darron was pissed off. Although he wasn't proud of what he was out on the streets doing, he relied on that money to help his mom out. He had already lied and told her that at night he helps stock and clean Eddie's store. He had his mom thinking that he was out here working two jobs, so coming home broke wasn't even an option.

"Man, fuck that shit. I say we go back in that bitch and get the rest of our bread. If we let this shit slide tonight, he'll get on fucking us over."

Marcus was surprised to see his childhood friend so amped up. "Bro, what you really wanna do?"

"Shid, I say let's go in that bitch and call that nigga out on his bullshit. I need all my bread. We're the ones out here in the streets risking our freedom while his ass sits up in the house feeding his nose and fucking that nasty hoe."

"You right, nigga, let's go back in that bitch."

Once they walked around to the back of the house, they could see that Sticks was slipping. They didn't even have to do their special knock because he had never got back up to lock the door behind Marcus. They walked right in and saw that he wasn't sitting at the table that was in the kitchen anymore. They could hear what sounded like sex noises coming from the living room. Walking straight in the room, not caring what was going on, the two friends witnessed Sticks' female friend bent over on the back of the couch getting fucked.

"Man, what the fuck y'all lil' niggas want?" He yelled without removing his dick from the dope fiend.

Darron, who at first was ready to confront the guy, was lost for words. Marcus, who was depending on his boy to stand up for the both of them, looked over towards his boy, hoping that any minute now he was going to say something.

"We...we came back in 'cause...'cause..." For some reason, the sight of the gun that Sticks had picked up from the couch made him pick back up his old stuttering problem from his childhood.

"We what, muthafucka? What the fuck you tryna say, boy?" Sticks yelled, putting more fear into the boys.

"Nothing, man," Marcus said, pulling at Darron.

"Come on, bro, let's get the fuck up outta here."

As they turned around to leave, they could hear the girl and Sticks laughing at them for being scary.

"Fuck that nigga, I got a plan," Marcus mumbled.

Darron stopped walking to hear his friend out. "What's up?"

"Let's snatch all this shit up and do this shit on our own. We ain't gotta keep working for his ass and have him play us like some bitches. He played us last time, but I just gave you whatever he gave us 'cause I knew you needed this shit more than me. So, you down?"

Before going their separate ways, they made a plan to hide the bag at Darron's house since his mom was gonna be already in bed when he got home and at work during the day. That way, they could figure out their next move. In their eyes, everything was gonna work out just fine.

Just as planned, Betty got up early to go to work, leaving Darron and Yaya home alone. Just like clockwork, Yaya was up around 9am, ready to eat and watch TV. After fixing her a bowl of cereal, Darron called Marcus to came over, so they could handle their business. Knowing that Yaya was nosy as hell and sometimes could be a snitch, he let her stay in the front room while he and Marcus went into his room.

"Man, I can't believe we got away with all this work."

"Hell yeah, bro, and he even bagged all the shit up for us," Darron said, laughing.

"So, what's the plan, bro?"

It only took Marcus a hot second to put shit together in his head, but he had a plan. "I say we take a few bags apiece and hit the blocks."

"Man, I don't know shit about that shit."

"So what, nigga? I do. I can show you. Did you forget that I be on these streets almost every day?" Marcus reminded him.

Darron wasn't sure about all that, but the desperate look in Marcus' eyes told him that he needed to have his boy's back.

"Alright, let me make sure Yaya straight, then we can bounce."

**A Few Blocks Away**

"I think you need to run that story back to me before I call Jackson over here, and you know ain't no talking when he gets here!" Rod yelled with his gun pointed at Sticks' head.

"I'm telling you the truth. Last night, those little niggas that I had working for me robbed me."

Rod slapped him upside the head with his gun.

"Shit not making sense to me, Sticks. How the fuck you get robbed by some little niggas? What the fuck was you doing when they were snatching Jackson's shit, muthafucka?"

Before Sticks could answer, James blurted out,

"That nigga lying to you, Rod! That nigga high as fuck right now off of Jackson's shit. Just look at that nigga, hehigh."

Rod pulled out his phone then dialed Jackson's number. "Hey, Boss Man. This nigga talking about those little niggas, Marcus and Darron, robbed him, but he sitting in my face right now high as giraffe's pussy."

Jackson didn't hesitate to give orders. "Handle his ass."

And just like that, Jackson hung up without a care in the world. Jackson was the father of three and although he had a business to run in the streets, his household came first.

"What's going on, baby?" Justice asked as she rolled over and rested her head on Jackson's chest.

"A knuckle head fucking up and had to be handled, that's it," he said, placing a kiss on her forehead.

"So, does that mean you gotta leave the house?" She asked.

Jackson put his hands under the bed sheet then placed her hand on his dick. "Do you feel how hard this muthafucka is? Do you think I'm about to leave this bed to fuck around with them fools in the streets?"

Justice giggled while moving her head down under the bed sheet. Jackson knew his wife was gonna take good care of him and make sure that every moment he spent in the house, he was completely satisfied.

"You like that, daddy?" Justice asked, licking around his tip.

"Hell yeah! Stop playing with it and suck that muthafucka up. You know how daddy like it, baby."

~

Just as planned, the boys hit the block that Marcus felt they would make the most money on.

"This shit tight, ain't it?"

"Hell yeah, bro. I'm almost out already and my pockets looking right," Darron admitted with a grin on his face.

While serving their customers, the boys never paid attention to the other cars that were riding up and down the block.

"Aye, Rod, ain't that them lil niggas over there that Sticks was talking about?"

Although Rod was driving, he tried to get a little peek across the street. "Hell yeah, that's them, and them niggas over there serving up."

"Damn, that nigga Sticks wasn't lying," James said, shaking his head.

"Man, fuck him. Any nigga that let some little niggas rob them deserves to die."

"I feel that. But what's our next move?"

"I'm gonna turn around and see what's up," Rod replied.

Just like he said, Rod turned around and made his way back towards the corner that Marcus and Darron were posted on. They parked then jumped out, trying to play shit cool. Marcus was just about to serve someone when Rod snatched the package out of his hand, causing the fien to run off.

"I know y'all little niggas ain't out here serving Jackson's stolen product."

Marcus knew what time it was and knew that they had fucked up. He wanted to fuck over Sticks so bad that he forgot all about the work really belonged to Jackson. Marcus turned towards Darron, who looked as if he was ready to shit on himself.

"Run, bro!" He yelled.

Darron hesitated for a second, but once Marcus yelled it out again, he took off. He had made it a block and a half away when he heard gun shots and his friend scream out in pain. He looked back in time to see his body hit the ground. Scared out his mind, Darron took back off, trying to make it to his house.

"Please God, I'm sorry, please help me!" He cried out as he ran home.

To her surprise, Betty was released from work early.

"Hey, Mommy!" Yaya yelled in full excitement. She was so happy to see her mama walking into the door.

"Hey, baby girl. Where that brother of yours at?"

"Mommy, he went to work with Marcus. He should be back soon so he can make my lunch and give me a snack."

Betty was all smiles. "Well since I'm here, I'm gonna take care of that and put dinner on for you and your hardworking brother."

"Can I help, please, Mommy?"

Betty placed a kiss on Yaya. "You sure can. We can make your brother's favorite meal tonight."

Yaya giggled. "Spaghetti, chicken and garlic bread."

"Yes, you're so right. You know your big brother so good. Now let's go into the kitchen and get you some lunch," Betty said, guiding Yaya towards the kitchen.

Before they could make it, the front door burst open.

"Boy, what the hell wrong with you?" Betty yelled, seeing her son quickly shutting the door and locking the locks.

"I'm so sorry, Ma, I'm so sorry!" He cried out.

"What's going on, Darron? What did you do?" Betty asked, grabbing her son and holding him in her arms.

Darron was hurt and was crying uncontrollably.

"They killed him, Ma. They killed Marcus."

"Marcus is dead?" Yaya quietly asked.

Betty looked towards her daughter. "Go to your room while I talk to your brother, Yaya," she ordered.

Yaya pretended to walk towards the back, but as soon as her mom's attention was back on her brother, she snuck into the closet that was in the front room. She was so nosy and needed to know all the details about the Marcus' murder. Betty didn't have all the details. but she knew her son had gotten into some mess.

"What happened, Darron?"

Through his tears, Darron tried to tell his mom what was going on. "Me and Marcus stole some drugs from the guy we were working for and now they're after us. I mean, they killed Marcus, Ma, and they're gonna come looking for me soon."

Betty instantly started to cry. "Oh no, Darron! I warned you about that street life shit. I told you that shit will only get you in trouble."

She then tried to calm down. She was more scared for his life than being mad that he had lied to her in the first place.

"Did they follow you here?"

"I don't know, ma, but we gotta get on."

Betty knew if she didn't think fast, she was only putting her family in greater danger. "Let me get my keys so we can go now."

Before she could make it out the front room, she heard the sound of her front door being kicked in full force.

"Where the fuck Jackson shit at, lil' nigga?" James asked, walking through the door with his pistol in his hand.

Betty threw herself in front of her son. "Look, I'll pay you whatever my son owes, just please don't hurt him," Betty begged and cried.

Rod, being a little meaner, wasn't trying to hear that shit. He slapped Betty across the face with his gun while yelling, "Bitch, shut the fuck up!"

Yaya wanted to scream out seeing her mama hit the floor, but she also was too afraid to climb out of the closet.

Without a second thought, Darron ran up on Rod, ready to defend his mama. His fist didn't even get a chance to connect to Rod's face before he was shot down.

"Stupid ass nigga!"

Betty, who was still on the ground, crawled over towards her dying son. As she cradled him in her arms, she repeatedly begged him not to die on her. "Please, Darron, fight. You gotta make it."

Darron stared his mama in the eyes then began to mumble. "I'm so sorry, ma. I love you and Yaya."

Darron had used the last breath in his body to tell his mom how he felt.

Betty panicked and started shaking her son. "Get up, Darron! Please, baby, get up!" She cried uncontrollable.

"Kill that bitch too, we don't need any witnesses."

Listening to Rod, James gave Betty a head shot, putting her down.

Yaya held her hands over her mouth, trying her hardest not to let her cries be heard by the bad men. She knew that if they found her hiding in the closet, she would be next to get killed. Rod and James ransacked the house looking for the drugs that Darron and Marcus had stolen. It was just their luck to find Darron's book bag hidden in his bedroom closet. While they were in the back of the house, Yaya ran out the front door and down the street to her mom's best friend Tonya's house. Before leaving out,

James and Rod had torched the house with the plans of getting rid of all evidence.

"What's wrong, baby?" Tonya asked, opening the door for the crying little girl that was standing on her porch.

"Call the police. They killed my mama and brother!" She cried out.

Tonya pulled the young girl into her home, but not before looking around and making sure no one had followed her down there. Tonya then sat Yaya down on the couch and went into the kitchen to grab her phone. Tonya quickly called the police and told them what Yaya said.

That day was the worst day of Yaya's life, and it was a day that she would never be able to forget.

# Chapter 3

**7 1/2 Years Later**

"Yaya!" Grandma Jean yelled out.

"Yes, Grandma, what's up?" Yaya responded.

"Girl, who you talking to like that? What I tell you about sass talking me?"

Yaya didn't mean any harm towards her grandma but quickly apologized. "Sorry, Grandma, it won't happen again."

Yaya was now 17 years old and ready to get away from her grandma. She did appreciate her taking her in after the death of her mom and brother, but it was hard living with a lady that didn't really care for her. The thing was, Grandma Jean hated her mom ever since she had got with their dad years ago. A lot of bad words were spoken and no one never apologized for anything. So, after years of not speaking to each other, Yaya's mom and grandma never had a chance to rekindle their relationship, and Grandma Jean never got a chance to meet her grandchildren before her death.

Over the years, Yaya was reminded of how her mom never listened to her grandma. She was also constantly reminded of how her dad did exactly what everyone told her mom he was gonna do and leave them. It was very clear that her grandma didn't give a fuck about her dad or mom, but to make matters worse, Granma didn't give a fuck about her either.

"Go in that kitchen and warm me up a can of that soup," she ordered.

"Yes, ma'am." As Yaya got up to leave, she could hear her grandma mumbling under her breath.

"Stupid bipolar black bitch."

Instead of responding or even trying to stand up for herself, Yaya cried her way into the kitchen. She knew that she would be graduating high school and turning 18 very soon, and she planned on leaving that house for good. She didn't know where she was going or what she was gonna do, but she was out. She could clearly understand why her mom left at a young age and never returned.

After giving her grandma her bowl of soup, Yaya returned to her room to finish her homework. Although she had been through such a tragic event in her life, Yaya managed to keep her grades up. The first year of going back to school after her mom and brother were murdered, she had fallen into depression and even skipped her classes a lot. It caused her to get bad grades, but her grandma was more than happy to beat it out of her. Classes that she was getting D's and F's in, she was now getting A's and B's in. Her grandma didn't believe in that whole therapy shit. She had her own way of handling things in her household. One thing that Yaya could look forward to was going to school. She had a couple of so-called friends and a best friend named Kiara that helped the time go by.

The next morning, Yaya got ready for school just like any other day. Right before she walked out the door, she went into her grandma's room.

"Granny, I'm gone, see you later."

"Gone head on, girl. You're interrupting my damn sleep!" Grandma Jean yelled.

Yaya walked out shaking her head. There was no reason in trying to be nice to that woman.

She made it four blocks away from her house before she met up with her best friend Kiara.

"What's up, girl?"

"Hey, boo, what's up? Did you study for Mrs. Brooke's English test?"

"Hell yeah, girl. You know I can't afford no bad grades on my transcript."

The girls continued to talk and make their way towards the school.

"Oh my God, girl! Did you see them sexy muthafuckas that just rode pass us?"

Yaya rolled her eyes. "Girl, no. Now you know I'm not paying these niggas out here know attention. My focus is on turning 18 and getting away from my grandma."

"Yaya, you tripping. Besides, that's not no random ass nigga. For your information, that's Jerrel's sexy black ass and his lil' brother, Jacques."

"Ok, bitch, you saying that like I know who that is," Yaya responded.

"Let me break some shit down for you, girl. Their daddy's name is Jackson. He used to run the whole east side back in the day, but now that nigga running the whole Detroit and surrounding areas. Anyways, them niggas right there got next whenever Jackson does decide to retire from these streets. Don't get me wrong, girl, from what I heard, Jerrel be putting in that work and making that bread too. Word around town is that he got a big ass dick. The only thing about that is he's not really the type to wife a bitch up, he just be wanting some pussy. Then Jacques is just like his ass. Neither one of them are looking for a bitch to settle down with right now. It's still a surprise that Jackson married their mom. I'm not gonna lie, if one of them niggas ever try to holler at me, I'm gonna become their personal porn star, and make them niggas wanna marry my ass. Girl, you better wake the fuck up."

Kiara was laughing, but Yaya hadn't heard too much after Jackson's name was mentioned. It had been years since she heard someone say that name in real life, but she had heard the guy who killed her family yell out his name every single day for the last 7 1/2 years.

"Hey, Ayanna, you ok, girl?"

"Yeah, I'm good, my bad."

"Anyways, I know your birthday is coming up. If you're not doing anything, which I know you're not, I'm going to this party in the hood this weekend. Do you think you'll be able make it?"

Yaya knew her grandma wasn't having that shit, but she really wanted to go out. "I'll let you know Friday."

"Ok, cool. I hope so 'cause we're gonna have so much fun."

Yaya gave her a fake smile but really wasn't really in the mood to be bothered anymore.

~

"Granny, you know my birthday is next week, right?" Yaya reminded her grandma with the hopes of actually being able to celebrate her birthday or even talking her into letting her hang with her friends that weekend.

"Child, I know when your birthday is. That's the day I'll never forget. Your mama called me from her hospital bed thinking I was gonna run my ass up there to see your little black ass because your no good daddy wasn't there. I laughed at her before hanging up on her sorry ass. You only here 'cause the state sends me a pretty penny to keep your ass."

Sometimes the insults didn't bother Yaya as much as they used to when she first moved in, but she hated hearing anything negative about her mama. Jumping up from the dinner table, Yaya stormed out of the kitchen and up the stairs to her room.

"Bring your black ass here, little black bitch!" Grandma Jean yelled.

"Fuck you!" Yaya yelled back, slamming her bedroom door.

Yaya had never disrespected her grandma up until that day, but she had finally had enough of her bullshit.

"You lucky I can't make it up those steps because I'll beat your ass real good, little girl. Your ass ain't grown yet, bitch."

Yaya sat on her bed crying. Over the years of staying with her grandma, she had heard so many stories that would have made others think that her mom was a bad person, but not Yaya. She only judged her mama based off the lady that she grew up with and loved so much. Her mother was her hero, right along with her big brother who she also loved so much. Nothing Grandma Jean said could ever make her think differently about them.

After a while, Yaya could hear her grandma's bedroom door close, so she knew that she was gonna be in the bed for the night. With a half ass plan, Yaya called Kiara to see if it would be alright if she spent the night over there. She had never been able to go over to her friend's house, let alone spend the night, but she was about to try her luck.

"Look, I know it's a school night, but I really need to get out of this house. My granny tripping on me."

"Girl, now you know you can. My mama likes you and her mean self don't like any of my friends," Kiara said, laughing

"Ok, cool. I'm about to be on my way over there."

Kiara agreed to meet her on the corner where they met up every day for school. Yaya grabbed her book bag and her gym bag that held some of her clothes and other personal items. She wasn't sure how long she was gonna be gone, but if she could, she would have made that night be her last night there.

~

Yaya looked around Kiara's front room. "Who all stays here with you?" She asked, thinking that the house seemed a little too cluttered.

"Girl, it's me, my mama, my auntie, and one of my cousins, but they come and go as they please. We deep in this bitch," Kiara said, laughing. Yaya wished that she had more family around. Just living with her grandma sucked.

That night, the girls stayed up late talking about what their plans were gonna be once they graduated from high school the following month.

"I'm so tired of Detroit, as soon as I graduate, I'm hitting the road. I'm trying to get far away from my family," Kiara admitted.

"Girl, I wanna get away from my grandma, but I'm not sure what I'm gonna do. To be honest, I need a fucking job."

"I got you, girl. I'm about to leave my job and buy my car. I'm cool with the owner, I can pull you in."

"Ok, cool, that'll be nice. Since I'm about to be 18, my grandma can't stop me from working. I still don't know why she never wanted me to work anyways."

Yaya lied. She knew exactly why her grandma never wanted to her to work. Grandma Jean was scared that she was gonna go running her mouth about how she was being treated. She didn't want that information to get to the wrong person, and then her checks would come to an end. It was always about the money just like she was told over the years. Then it could have been that Grandma Jean just didn't want Yaya to be independent with her own money and leave the way her mama did.

"Girl, I been told you that I could get you a job at the clothing store where I work. Besides, I told them that I was leaving after graduation anyways."

~

Usually the school hours would have dragged and made Yaya feel as if she had been there 20 hours straight, but that Friday, she was glad that time flew by.

After school, the girls went straight to Kiara's job. For the last year or so, she had been working at a nice little boutique called Glamorous Girl. She got along with everyone there and knew that they would love Yaya.

"Hey, Kiara, I didn't know you worked today," a cashier name Ashley called out as Kiara and Yaya walked in.

"Girl, I don't, thank the Lord," she replied, laughing. Kiara then turned back to talk to Yaya. "Girl, wait right here, let me go get Mrs. Justice."

"Wait, who is that?"

"Girl, she the head bitch in charge. Don't worry, she's cool."

Yaya nervously waited for Kiara and Ms. Justice to walk out from the back. She had no job experience, so she had a feeling that she wasn't gonna get the job. She just prayed Kiara's word of mouth helped pull her in.

"Ms. Justice, this is my best friend Ayanna. I'm telling you she can get the job done and she's pretty, so she'll help the store out. You only want pretty chicks working in here, right?"

Ms. Justice gave Yaya a look over. "Ok, ok, I see you, girl," she said, smiling. She then turned her attention back to Kiara. "She is pretty and her beautiful brown skin is winning me over. I swear she reminds me of my baby Jewel. So, Yaya, when can you start?"

"Dang, Ms. Justice, I haven't even left yet," Kiara jokingly said.

"I know, baby, but who the hell you think is gonna train her? You know I don't be here like that and besides, you got it, girl. You can run this store by yourself."

Yaya went into the back office to fill out the proper paperwork. She was now gonna be a working woman. After leaving the boutique, the girls headed to Kiara's house. They wanted to chill before the party.

"Aye, Kiara, have you seen my black Polo shirt?" Kiara's older cousin asked as he walked into her room.

Both Kiara and Yaya looked up from the TV. Yaya wasn't tryna be rude and stare, but his face looked so familiar.

"Nah, I ain't seen shit, now get out my room."

"Man, why the hell you gotta be so mean?"

"Get out!" Kiara yelled.

He then pulled out a knot from his pocket. "I was gonna give you some money but fuck you then."

Kiara jumped out of the bed. "Wait a minute, lil' ugly, run me some of that."

He walked out of the room, not paying her any attention. She followed right behind him.

"So, you really about to make me chase you for some money, Rod?"

Stopping in the living room, Rod finally turned to face his lil' cousin. "Hook me up with your girl, and I got you."

"My girl not like those hoes you're used to fucking with. To be honest, she's a good girl and never even had a nigga before."

Rod smiles. "Even better. That's how I like them," he said, licking his lips.

"Nasty bastard."

Rod started thumbing the stack in his hand while Kiara watched him.

"Man, I'll see what I can do," she said before walking back into her room.

Returning to the room, Kiara saw Yaya grabbing her clothes.

"What you doing, boo?"

"I'm gonna jump in the shower and get ready for this party."

"Oh, ok, cool. So anyways, my cousin wanna holler at you."

Yaya gave her a strange face. "Girl, that nigga old as hell, what the fuck."

Kiara wanted that money bad, so she tried to vouch for her cousin. "Girl, that nigga only 27 years old. Plus, he be making bread in these streets. You better jump on it before another bitch catch his attention."

Yaya knew right then that Kiara wasn't shit. And with that in her mind, she had no problem playing out her next move.

"Let me shower and think about it."

Kiara was all smiles now. "Ok, boo, welcome to the family," she jokingly said.

Yaya smiled then walked out of the room and into the bathroom.

Kiara went into the basement where Rod now lived. She had kind of stretched the truth about Rod. That nigga used to get money in the streets, but now he was barely making it. He was what the new guys called washed up and a has been.

"Man, what that bitch talking about?" He asked.

"First of all, don't call my girl out her name. How the fuck you gon' get a girl being disrespectful like that? I told you she ain't used to all that, so don't scare her off, fool."

"My bad," Rod said, feeling stupid.

"She said let her think about it."

"Man, I ain't got that much time. I gotta go see Nikki tonight. She been bitching about me not spending enough time with her and Jr."

"Oh well, nigga, no new pussy for you, stupid ass."

Kiara snatched some money from off his table then made her way back upstairs. Opening up the door, she saw that Yaya was standing there with a big T-shirt on.

"Girl, I don't know what the fuck I'm gonna wear tonight."

"If you don't have shit to wear, look thru my closet. My checks be going straight back to that boutique. Ms. Justice be having all the nice shit in there."

Yaya smiled. "Ok, girl."

"So, have you thought about my cousin? That nigga really wanna holler at you, girl."

"Yeah, but I don't think I'm ready for all that right now," Yaya replied.

"Oh, ok." Kiara started grabbing her stuff. "I need to take a long, hot shower, so I'll be back in a few."

Once Kiara was in the bathroom, Yaya put her plan in action. She quietly snuck downstairs into the basement.

"What you doing down here?" Rod asked.

Yaya took a seat on the edge of his bed. She slowly opened her legs, exposing her freshly shaved pussy. "I heard you were asking about me."

Rod had always been a sucker for pretty bitches with pretty pussies. He was hypnotized at first sight. "Damn, baby girl," he mumbled, walking towards the bed.

Yaya didn't have much experience with guys but knew her own body all too well. She lay back enough to still be able to see Rod's face disappear in between her legs. She fought hard not to enjoy his tongue inside her but ended up letting out a few moans, begging him for more. Just as her leg began to shake and she was on the verge of cumming, she pushed him off her and closed her legs.

"What's wrong, baby?" He asked, trying to open her leg back up.

"Look, I gotta go get ready for this party your cousin is dragging me to, but maybe we'll meet up sometime soon."

Rod rubbed his dick. "Damn, baby girl, you got me rock hard. I need that shit right now. You tasted so fucking good, I can't wait."

As he tried to kiss her, Yaya turned her head. She couldn't believe that after all these years, she had finally ran into one of the muthafuckas that were responsible for fucking up her once so perfect life.

"I told you I had to go, I'll be back later," she said, rubbing his dick thru his pants.

Yaya made it back upstairs right before Kiara came out the shower.

"I see your ass still ain't got dressed yet."

"I was thinking about wearing this dress, what you think?"

"Hell no, girl. A house party with a bunch of horny ass guys drinking? That's not a good look," Kiara reminded her.

Yaya giggled as she picked up a pair of black jeans that had a few cuts in them. "How about these?"

"Yes, bitch! Not too fancy but show a little skin. I'll say those are perfect."

The girls giggled as they got dressed for the party.

"So did my cousin come up here fucking with you?"

"Nah, but I did hear the front door shut. Maybe he left."

"Good, 'cause that nigga can be nerve wrecking." Yaya smiled but didn't say anything. She peeped game already.

It wasn't long before they were walking out the house a few blocks from hers.

"Man, my mom gone, so tonight. I'm tryna get fucked up. I kind of wish I saw Lance at the party, especially since Rod left. Nobody will be at the house but us. Maybe Lance could spend the night and fuck the shit out of me like he did a week ago."

Yaya laughed. "I see you got everything planned out."

"Yeah, you just gon' have to sleep on the couch, boo."

"I have no problem with that. As long as I'm not at home with my granny's mean ass," Yaya said as they reached their destination.

Yaya has always been on lock down, so it took her a minute to adjust to being around so many people at once. Soon as they walked in, they were greeted by people from their school. To Yaya's surprise they were also handed drinks. Wanting to be in the right mind when it was time to handle her business, Yaya held her cup but never sipped out of it. She couldn't let this opportunity slip away from her.

"Oh my God, bitch. Lance's sexy ass is over there," Kiara said with her words slurring.

"Go holler at your dick then," Yaya said, hoping that she would get the fuck on.

"Man, I don't wanna leave you over here by yourself."

Yaya gave her a funny look. "It's a thousand muthafuckas in here, girl. Trust me, I'm good. I'm about to go mingle with some of these muthafuckas. Please don't let me stop you from having fun, I swear I don't need a babysitter."

"Ok, boo, but let's set some rules first. Ok, look, we can't leave without telling the other one and we meet back in front in about an hour just to check in."

"In an hour… ok, cool."

Kiara walked away to go talk to her boo. She looked back as she made it across the room and saw that Yaya was already gone. She wondered where she had gone to that quick, but with Lance kissing on her, she forgot all about it that fast.

Yaya was on a mission and didn't have much time to stand around. She jogged and ran back to Kiara's house. Once she got there, she wondered how she was gonna get in unnoticed. After a minute or so, she walked around to the back of the house then knocked on the basement window. Rod sat up from his weight bench. As he walked closer towards the window, he saw that it was Yaya.

"Go to the back door!" He yelled out the window.

Soon as he opened up the door, he picked her up and carried her back downstairs. She tried so hard not to throw up in her mouth as he kissed all over her and palmed her ass.

"I was hoping you came back to me."

"I told you I was. I needed to see you more than you could ever know."

He continued to kiss on her and pull her clothes off, never really understanding what she meant by that.

Once again, Rod had his face buried in between her legs, enjoying every single drop of her pussy juices that touched his tongue.

"Stop running and cum for me," he ordered.

Yaya didn't say anything, but she knew that it was only a matter of time before she soaked his bed up.

"Y'all young bitches be sitting on a fucking gold mine and don't even know it."

Yaya started moaning out louder as he slowly lifted her up. He put her in a position so that his tongue could now easily rub against her asshole. She had heard about niggas like him from females at school. These older guys would hook up with a young girl and turn her ass out just so she would only chase after his dick, no matter if he had a main bitch or not. Rob was doing a good job, but Yaya was a different type of bitch and on a mission. She wasn't into chasing behind a dead nigga. Right before filling him mouth up with her juices, Yaya started pushing Rod off her.

"Please, baby, don't do that shit again. Let me taste all of that," he begged.

Yaya was shaking as she had her first orgasm that she didn't bring to herself.

"Yes!" She moaned out.

Rod wasn't trying to get her in her emotions or anything, but he was ready to fuck. He wiped his mouth off with the back of his hand as he climbed on top of her shaking body.

"I'm about to make you feel so good," he whispered into her ear.

Rod almost caught Yaya slipping. She quickly pushed him off her.

"Man, what the fuck is your problem?" He yelled, climbing off her.

Yaya quickly got back into character. "Let me make you happy, daddy." Standing up from the bed, Yaya guided him over to the workbench that was across the room. "Shut up, lay back and let me take control."

Rod wanted to question why they couldn't use the bed but, decided to go with the flow.

"Alright, baby girl, you got it. Damn, you so fucking pretty and your body is amazing. Kiara told me that you never been with a nigga before, but the way you trying to take control, I seriously doubt that," he said before laying back.

"Didn't I tell you to be quiet?" She asked while spotting the perfect weapon. She tried not to let what Kiara told him bug her at that moment.

Rod laid on the bench, waiting to feel her insides on his dick, but didn't mind her sliding back down on his face. Yaya hated that she was enjoying the head way too much. She kept forgetting that she was on a mission and the hour that she had was counting down.

"Hey, Rod, didn't you use to work for a nigga name Jackson?" She asked as she slowly climbed off his face then started kissing on his chest, working her way down towards his dick.

"Hell yeah. Matter of fact, I still do a little something something from time to time."

Rod was so caught up from the head that Yaya was giving him, he never opened his eyes to see what she was doing. All he knew was that her mouth was wet and warm just the way he liked it.

"Have you ever killed for him?"

"It's all a job, baby girl. What's with all these questions? Just worry about making that dick cum before I gotta meet my baby mama."

That's what really pissed Yaya off. Her mother and brother's death were just a fucking job to him. She didn't give a fuck about that last comment about his baby mama at all.

"Come on, baby girl, why you acting like you scared to put this dick in you?"

"Maybe I am."

"What you scared of? I'm not gonna hurt you," Rod said, sounding like her really gave a fuck about how she felt.

A tear fell from her eyes. "You're a killer, Rod," she mumbled.

"Ok, cool. Now that we both know that, let me go ahead and kill that pussy."

It was a second of silence before Rod looked at Yaya and saw her face. "Fuck wrong with you, girl?"

"You're a fucking murderer!"

Not knowing what her problem was, Rod tried to push her head back down on his dick.

"Go ahead and handle your business," he ordered.

Yaya kissed to tip and with that move, he closed his eyes again. She knew he was right and needed to handle her business soon. She stopped sucking on his dick long enough to pick up the weight. It was heavier than she needed it to be, but with all the anger built up in her, she managed to pick it up enough to drop it right on his fucking neck. She watched as his body squirmed around, and he tried to get it off him. Her move had caught him off guard, and he was having a hard time lifting the weight off of him. Scared that he wasn't dying fast enough, she tried to push the weights down even more.

"About 8 years ago, you and that bitch ass nigga James killed my mama and brother as I hid in the fucking closet. You took away the only people that will ever love me. And for that, I have to make sure you never breathe again."

Rod tried moving his mouth as if he wanted to say something to her, but he suddenly stopped moving. Yaya jumped off him with a face full of tears. She was scared, only because that was her first kill. At the same time, she was happy that she got it out the way. Taking an old towel that was down there, she started wiping down everything that she thought she touched. Watching a bunch of TV shows, she knew that they could find her DNA, so she grabbed the bleach from the laundry room then poured it down his throat. Looking at the time on her phone, she knew that it was time for her to get back to the party. Using the towel, Yaya turned the bottom lock then shut the back door behind her.

The next morning, Kiara woke up with a slight hangover, but the dick that Lance served her was just what she begged for. She climbed out of bed to grab a pill and bottle of water.

"Aye, girl, you straight?" She asked Yaya who was lying on the couch.

"Yeah, girl, I'm good. If anything, I should be asking if you're good. I heard y'all in there all night. I'm surprised he got up to leave early this morning."

Kiara returned from the kitchen then took a seat on the couch by Yaya's feet. "Girl, I'm so in love with that boy, and that's not just because of the dick either."

"I can't wait to find the one to make me feel like I'm on top of the world. I wanna have a big family one day."

"It could have been my cousin, but I bet his baby mama probably called him back to the house. She be using that baby to trap him, and he falls for it every time."

Yaya really didn't give a fuck about what she was talking about. Little did Kiara know, her perverted ass cousin was in the basement dead. She smiled and pretended to be ok hearing Kiara run her mouth about her hoe ass cousin.

# Chapter 4

Yaya had been gone since Thursday night and knew that she was about to hear her grandma mouth. As she opened the door and walked into the living room, she was surprised to hear her grandma yell out for her.

"Hey, Yaya, how was school?"

Grandma Jean gave her a funny look as the social worker stood up to greet Yaya. Knowing all too well how to behave when they had company, especially from the state, she smiled.

"Hey, Granny."

"Ayanna, please take a seat so that we can discuss what's next for you," Mrs. Taylor said.

Yaya took a seat on the love seat. "What's going on, Granny?"

"Chile, just listen to the lady."

Mrs. Taylor began to talk as she shuffled through some papers. "Ok, with your 18th birthday approaching in two days, I stopped by to talk about your case. As you know, in two days, you would be considered an adult, which means that whatever your mom left for you following her death will now be in your possession.

Yaya was dumbfounded. "What do you mean? My mom left me something?" She questioned.

The social worker looked over towards Grandma Jean, wondering why she never told Ayanna about her mother leaving her anything, but didn't say anything.

"Yes, young lady. Now if you want, we can keep things like they are, or we can have everything in your name."

Before Yaya could say anything, Grandma Jean answered for her. "I believe everything is fine just the way they are. Me and Yaya have such a great bond and routine with her funds, I don't see no need to change the way that things are now. What's that old saying? If it ain't broke, don't try to fix it."

Mrs. Taylor and Grandma Jean laughed, but Yaya couldn't believe how fake her Grandma was acting.

"Nah, I want any and everything that my mom left me in my name ASAP."

Grandma Jean's eyes got big. "Baby, are you sure?"

"Positive. Now if we're done here, I need to change for work."

Mrs. Taylor handed over a few forms that Yaya needed to sign before heading out the door. It was settled, Yaya was now her in control of her own funds.

"You know what, little girl, no matter what, I raised you and you can't just disappear when you want to. Matter of fact, when you get that money, you need to look out for me 'cause I spent years taking care of your black ass."

"Fuck outta here with that. My mama's money took care of me, so gone somewhere with that shit."

"You think 'cause you about to be grown you can talk to me any old way?"

"You been dogging me my whole fucking life, even before you met me," Yaya cried. She tried not to let her feelings get in her way, but her grandma had a way of bringing them out. "Do you know how hard it was for me to witness my brother get shot down and then my mama cradling his body, begging him not to die, just for a muthafucka to shoot her next like she didn't mean shit to anybody? I witnessed that shit and it plays in my mind every single day. It was so hard to meet you for the first time after hearing my mom say that you were dead. Once I got here, I thought you were gonna love me. But to you, I was just a little black bitch that came with a fucking paycheck."

As Yaya cried, she sat back down on the couch and rocked herself, trying to calm down. To her surprise, her grandma walked over towards her and just held her in her arms. Yaya wasn't sure if it was because of the money she was about to get or if her grandma was finally coming around, but that hug felt good. She hadn't felt a real hug since that day her family was taken from her. As she could remember, her mom hugged her as soon as she walked in the door from work.

~

Yaya had called Kiara three times before catching the bus to the boutique. She knew she was supposed to get trained that day and was scared to get there before Kiara. As she walked in, she saw Ms. Justice talking to a young lady that had to be around her age.

"Good, Yaya, you're here. Kiara said she had a family emergency and couldn't come in to train you today, but I called my daughter in to help out."

"Family emergency? Is everything ok?"

"I'm not sure, honey, but I'll give her a call later."

The young lady that Ms. Justice was talking to walked over towards them. "Hi, I'm Jewel and I'll be showing you the ropes around the store."

Yaya smiled. "Hi, Jewel. I'm Ayanna but everyone calls Yaya."

"Ok, ladies, please let today go smoothly. I need to get home and put dinner on for your father."

The young ladies watched as she grabbed her purse then walked out.

"Before we start, do you mind if I call Kiara? Your mom mentioned a family emergency and I'll feel so bad if I didn't check on her."

"Sure, go ahead. Besides, Ashley's running the register and we are stocking up, which is so much better than the register if you asked me."

Jewel then walked towards some boxes of clothes that were sitting out. Yaya took out her phone as she watched Jewel pull out some t-shirts.

"Hello."

"Kiara, what's going on?"

Kiara cried into the phone. "Yaya, Rod is dead."

"Oh no, Kiara, what happened?" She asked, pretending to care.

"I don't know. All I know is that I went downstairs to wash my clothes. Something told me to go on his side and he was dead."

"Oh my God, Kiara. I'm at the boutique but if you need me, I'll leave right now."

"No, girl. You need that job, don't leave because of this. Plus, it ain't too much you can do here. I'll call you later."

"Kiara, if you need anything, please call me."

"Ok, Yaya. Thanks for being a friend."

Yaya put her phone back into her back pocket then walked over towards Jewel. "Where do I start?"

"Just make sure these shirts are folded up neatly and stack them like this at a slight angle." Jewel showed her what to do and Yaya was ready to work.

"There are some pretty ass clothes in here."

"Yes, girl, and I get whatever I want."

"Of course, your mom's the boss, why wouldn't you?"

"Honestly, my mom is the boss, but my dad owns all these little businesses around here. That barbershop, that chicken joint over there and that car wash."

"Damn, really? That's nice," Yaya said, impressed.

Yaya had been working for damn near two hours when a guy walked in that she was sure she saw around.

"Jewel, what y'all eating on today?" He called out.

Yaya turned away. She knew someone that handsome had to be there for the boss's daughter.

"Let me ask the new girl what she likes, you already know what Ashley wants."

Jewel walked over towards where Yaya was working at. "Hey, what do you want for lunch?"

"I'm not sure, shit, I only got $5 on me."

Jewel started to giggle. "My brother gets our lunch, girl. I told you, we all family over here. So, do you like chicken or fish?"

"Chicken."

Yaya then watched as Jewel went back up front to her brother. "Get us two chicken dinners and one fish. All with fruit punches. Jerrel, do you hear me?" She yelled out.

Yaya had Jerrel's attention at the moment. He hadn't heard shit Jewel said.

"Jerrel," Jewel called out again.

"My bad, sis, what was that again?" Jerrel said, trying to pull his eyes away from Yaya.

Jewel rolled her eyes as she repeated her order. "Two chicken, one fish, all with fruit punch to drink."

"Yeah, ok, I got it, but who is shorty back there?"

"Boy, we hungry, and you worried about who that is?" Jewel jokingly asked.

Being petty, Jewel turned around to get Yaya's attention. "Hey, Yaya, you have to come place your order with my big bro."

Jerrel gave his baby sister a funny look.

"You need to be thanking me, now y'all can talk, butthead," Jewel said before walking away.

Yaya tried to fix her shirt as she walked towards Jerrel. He was handsome and she instantly wanted to meet him.

"Hey."

"Hey. What did you wanna eat for lunch? We got fish, chicken, burgers, and fries."

"You can just give me some chicken, thank you," she shyly said.

Jewel wasn't too far away. "I told his ass two chickens and one fish. I don't know why he acts like you had to tell him yourself."

Yaya laughed at Jewel, but she could tell that Jerrel was embarrassed. Jerrel always had women throwing themselves at him, and now there stood a pretty browned skinned girl that he couldn't stop staring at. This time, he wanted to throw himself at her. He couldn't remember seeing her around, so he figured that she hadn't been passed around the hood.

"Man, I'll be back in a few with y'all lunch."

Jewel and Yaya watched as Jerrel walked out.

"Girl, what you do to my brother?" Jewel asked with a huge grin on her face.

"Nothing, this was honestly my first time meeting him."

Jewel started to laugh. "Girl, you got that fool nose wide open. He wants you."

"He don't even know me, girl."

They continued to work and get the store stocked back up for the week. Jewel wasn't surprised when her other bother, Jacques, walked into the boutique with their food forty minutes later.

"Aye, Jerrel told me to drop this off."

Jewel giggled. "I bet he did. Tell that fool I said don't be scared."

Yaya put her head down, trying not to laugh at Jewel.

"Whatever, with your annoying, spoiled ass," Jacques snapped.

"I'm not annoying and I'm telling daddy what you called me."

Jacques pretended to shiver as if he was scared in his boots. "Ain't anybody scared."

Jewel didn't say anything else as she watched him walk out of the store.

"Yaya, I swear I'm glad you here to see how annoying my brothers are. They been driving me crazy my whole life."

Jewel handed Yaya her food before taking Ashley hers. Yaya didn't expect for her first day to be this funny, but it also made her think about her brother. She probably would have been bugging Darron and then threatening to tell their mom when he said something to her. Her life deserved to be so much better than what it was. She deserved a chance to have a good laugh with her mom and brother.

Yaya was walking out the door when she was approached by Jerrel.

"Aye, Yaya, how you getting home tonight?"

"The same way I got here."

"Why get smart, shorty? I was just trying to be helpful."

"Sorry, and you're right. Anyways, I was on my way to the bus stop," Yaya responded.

"Can I give you a ride home?"

Yaya blushed a little as she debated if she was gonna get in his car or not. It was hard for her to fully understand guys sometimes. Most just wanted a quick nut. And then with her growing up thinking that she was so black and ugly, she never knew who wanted what from her.

"I live kind of far from here."

Jerrel chuckled. "I didn't ask you all that. Besides, I got gas money," Jerrel said, opening up the passenger side door. Yaya got into the car, ready to get home. Although her job was easy, she was tired of unloading all of them boxes of clothes.

Once Jerrel got in and started his car, the loud music started to bang out of the speakers, causing Yaya to jump in her seat.

"My bad, shorty," he said, turning his music down.

At first, the ride was quiet then Jerrel finally started talking to Yaya. "So, I've been driving around for a minute now, and you ain't told me where you live at."

Yaya slowly opened her eyes. She hadn't even noticed that she had started to fall asleep. "My bad, I was tired."

"I see," he laughed, but things got quiet again. "I guess you don't wanna go home then. Where you tryna go, shorty?"

"My bad, I'm so tired that I feel lost right now. Don't think I'm slow."

"I don't. I actually think you're sexy as hell and that smooth, dark skin you got is a major turn on. It actually works so well with my black skin. It's like Melanin magic."

Yaya giggled. She had never heard anyone say such a nice thing about her dark skin since her mom died. She had always been teased about it in school, and now with her grandma.

"You're so silly, Jerrel."

"Tell me about yourself, I wanna get to know you. So far, all I know is that your name is Yaya. I'm sure that not your real name, and I know you work with my mom and my little sister."

"It ain't much to tell. My real name is Ayanna. I'll be 18 in two days and that's it."

"What you doing for your birthday?" Jerrel asked, using this opportunity to ask her out.

"I don't really celebrate my birthday. Growing up in a household with only my grandma, we didn't really do holidays and shit like that," Yaya admitted.

"Damn, shorty, that's fucked up. Would it be a problem if I took you out and showed you a good time? You're about to be 18, girl, you gotta want to do something."

Yaya paused. "I don't know you all like that."

"But you took a ride from me and we been riding around for half an hour now. Don't you think if I wanted to do something to you, it would have happened by now?"

Yaya giggled then got serious. "I guess you're right, but I think it's time for you to take me home so my granny won't be tripping on me."

"Ok, cool, but think about what I asked you. I don't mean any harm, I just wanna show you a good time and see what you about."

"Ok, I'll think about it."

After telling Jerrel were she stayed, he turned his car in that direction. He enjoyed riding around with her and just talking. It had actually been a minute since he could chill with a female without her begging for something. Just because of who his daddy was, most females would have already had him pull over to serve them some dick. Maybe Yaya was what he had been missing this whole time.

"So, this is your place?" He asked as he pulled up to her grandma's house.

"Yeah, this is my granny's place and my place of residency until my birthday. For my birthday, I'll be getting my own apartment or something."

"Big plans for the birthday girl."

Yaya wanted to get out of the car and go inside before her grandma embarrassed her, but she was in the middle of having a stare off with Jerrel, which soon turned into them sharing a kiss. As they finally separated, Jerrel tried to pull her back closer towards him, but she wasn't having it.

"Ok, that's enough, Jerrel."

"My bad, but why you stop?" He questioned.

"We don't know each other like that, and I'm not sure what you think about me, but I'm not some little hoe fucks just anybody."

Jerrel laughed. "Nah, I really didn't see you as that type, ma. I just thought that it felt right to do at the moment. I thought we both were feeling it and wanted it to happen. Plus, it felt nice."

Yaya opened her door. "See you, and thanks for the ride, Jerrel."

"Wait, Yaya!" He called out.

Yaya turned and climbed back into the car. "Yes, Jerrel?"

"Can you at least put your number in my phone so I can hit you up?"

Yaya took his phone out of his hand then put her number in it. Jerrel quickly called the number and waited for her phone to ring.

"Really, Jerrel?" Yaya laughed, hearing her phone go off.

"I had to make sure I wasn't getting played," he said, laughing.

Yaya laughed as she got back out the car.

Soon as she got into the house, she went to her grandma's room. "Hey, Granny, are you alright?"

"Yeah, I'm good. How was your first day at work?"

Yaya was surprised that she asked about her day but didn't mind telling her that the job seemed perfect. After talking to her for a minute, she went upstairs to her room.

"Oh, shit!" She said as she remembered that she needed to text Kiara.

*Yaya: Hey, boo, I was just thinking about you. If you need someone to talk to, I'm here.*

*Kiara: Hey, I'm alright, just trying to help my auntie keep her head up. That was her oldest child.*

Yaya rolled her eyes. She really didn't give a fuck how anyone was feeling over Rod's death. Her brother was her mama's only boy and oldest child, so fuck him and whoever felt like she was wrong. Rod got exactly what he deserved in her eyes.

*Yaya: I know, tell everyone I'm praying for them.*

*Kiara: I will, and I'll let you know when the funeral is.*

Yaya put her phone down on her bed. She was real life tired and just wanted to jump in the shower then straight into bed. Plus, she had school in the morning and knew it was gonna be a drag.

~

Twenty minutes later, Jerrel jumped out the car after pulling into the driveway. He was glad the night was coming to an end 'cause he was tried as hell. He had already been off work, but he stuck around waiting for Yaya to get of work from the boutique. At first glance, she had caught his attention, and he just had to have her to himself. He'd never been pressed about a female before, but it was something about Yaya that made him wanna know her a little better.

Since Jerrel could remember, he had been helping out with their family businesses. Although his dad had bread and was known as this big-time drug dealer back in the day, he had this thing where he didn't want his kids in the streets like he was growing up. So instead, he invested his money into different businesses, that way his money was clean and his family never would have to worry about finances. His dad still had muthafuckas working for him, just not his own seeds.

"What's up, Jacques? Why the fuck your ass on the couch and not in your room sleep?"

Jacques sat up. "I was blowed as fuck and dozed off for a second. What's good, bro?"

Jerrel took a seat next to his baby brother. "I guess your ass too blowed to hit this bitch then?" He asked, holding up a nice, fat Kush blunt.

"You got me fucked up. Light that bitch up."

The brothers got into rotation and discussed their day just like any other day.

"Man, you see that new lil bitch that works at the boutique with Jewel?"

"Hell yeah, bro. That's all me, I already called it," Jerrel called out with a weird grin on his face.

"Nigga, fuck you. Your ass always trying to claim these hoes first. The way these hoes act all crazy about us, we both might can get her."

"Whatever, nigga. She not even that type. I'm telling you, she different, bro. She ain't like them other sack-chasing hoes that's after dick and money."

"And how you figure that? You just met the girl today." Jacques asked. He couldn't believe how his brother was acting over a chick that he had just met.

"I took her home after work tonight, and we were able to just chill and talk. Baby girl got a good head on her shoulders."

"She sucked your dick, nigga?" Jacques yelled, acting foolish.

Jerrel snatched his blunt from Jacques. "Give me my shit back. Yeah, nigga you done for the night."

Jacques didn't say shit else as his brother walked away. He was already blowed, so he didn't give a fuck. Besides he had his own weed anyways.

~

The next morning, Jerrel woke up with Yaya on his mind. He even had stored her number in his phone as Pretty Brown Baby.

After a hot shower, he sat on the edge of his bed with his towel wrapped around his waist, just holding his phone, debating if it was too soon to call Yaya. He ain't never been the one to chase behind a bitch, but like he told his brother, she was different.

Just as her phone started to ring, he was sent straight to voicemail.

"What the fuck? This girl don't know who the fuck I am or something," he mumbled.

Soon as he was about to toss the phone on the bed, a notification was sent to his phone, telling him that someone had sent him a message. He grinned seeing that it was Yaya hitting him back up.

*Yaya: Can't talk right now. I'm in class, but I can text. What's up?*

Jerrel shook his head. Just that quick, he forgot that she was a few years younger than him. Jerrel was only 23 and she was one day shy of being 18, so he really wasn't on no R. Kelly type of shit. He quickly texted her back.

*Jerrel: Just seeing how you're doing. Can I pick you up from school so we can chill later?*

Yaya blushed before telling him exactly where and when he could pick her up. She still couldn't believe that he was interested in her, but she was ready to finally live her life. Yaya wanted to tell Kiara the good news, but because of the death of her cousin, she stayed home that day. So, while on her lunch break, she decided to text Kiara to check in on her. She was gonna play the concerned friend role first, then she was gonna bring up the good news.

*Yaya: Hey, boo, how are you holding up?*

*Kiara: Hey, girl. I'm good, just trying to wrap my head around all this shit. I miss my cousin so much. He was irritating sometimes, but he always looked out for me.*

*Yaya: Aww, boo. I'm so sorry about this and wish I could take the pain away.*

*Kiara: Anyways, how was your first day on the job?*

*Yaya: It was great. I worked with Ashley and Jewel, they seemed cool. For what it was, I really enjoyed it.*

*Kiara: Did you meet Jerrel and Jacques' sexy asses?*

*Yaya: Double yes, bitch. Them brothers know they fine as hell.*

*Kiara: They both sexy just like their fucking daddy. I'll lick up all that chocolate sauce they dripping.*

Yaya laughed. Even dealing with death, her friend was still silly as ever.

*Yaya: Girl, you talking like I know who they daddy is. I only met them yesterday.*

*Kiara: I swear you don't be listening to me when I be talking to you. I told your ass before that their daddy is a nigga named Jackson. He own all that shit, so you'll be seeing him soon.*

Yaya read over that text a million times and the name Jackson jumped out at her. Yaya became angry at herself for even forgetting who Jerrel's father was. Not worrying about texting Kiara back, she tossed her phone into her back pocket then ate her lunch.

For the rest of the school day, she thought about how she was gonna act around him, and how she could also use this as an advantage to take out him and his whole family. Maybe being the bitch that he wanted would work out in her favor. It was time to put her plan into action.

Jerrel parked his car in front of the school, waiting on Yaya to walk out of the building. He laughed seeing all the girls watching him, trying to see who he was up there picking up. They weren't sure who the girl was, but they knew she was a lucky bitch. He chuckled as he watched some of the niggas hug on their bitch, scared that he was up there choosing a new one. It was crazy how insecure niggas became whenever he or his bother came around. Little did they know, at that moment, he only had his eyes on one girl.

# Chapter 5

"I can't believe you got me skipping school to hang with you, boy," Yaya said, climbing into Jerrel's car.

After spending a few hours with him the day before after school, he convinced her that he needed more of her time. That conversation ended with him talking her into skipping school to spend her whole birthday with him.

"I told you I was gonna make sure this would be the best birthday ever. Now put your seatbelt on and let me make shit happen."

Yaya never had been the hardheaded type, so she did as she was told. "Ok, sir," she jokingly teased.

"Since we got that out the way, ain't shit about me a boy. I'm a grown ass man, just to let you know."

"Ok, grown man, you got it." Yaya wanted to say some smart shit but right now, her plan was to make him want her before she ended his whole family's existence.

"So, what's the plan for today?"

"I'm not sure about everything, but I wanna start the day off right by treating you to breakfast."

"Ok, I can go for that. You're so nice, Jerrel. What you want with a girl like me?"

Jerrel was caught off guard by her question. "Fuck you mean? I don't think you know just how beautiful you really are. You can't blame me for wanting to make you mine. You not the type that sits around me only wanting to talk about money and shit. From what I got out of you, you're very smart and I like that."

Although Yaya blushed at his confession, her brain kept telling her that she better not fall for his shit. His family was her enemies. Jerrel noticed how she got quiet.

"And that's another thing, you look so pretty playing that shy role. That shit really is turning me on," he admitted.

"Thank you, Jerrel, you're so sweet. To be honest, you're really one of the first guys to appreciate a girl like me. I guess that's why I questioned what your attentions were with me."

Jerrel shook his head. "That's understandable, ma."

Jerrel didn't hear her say the exact words but knew by what she said, he was right about her being different from the other hoes that he dealt with.

After breakfast, Jerrel took Yaya on a little shopping spree. She had never been able to walk into a store and just go crazy buying clothes, shoes and accessories. Her grandma gave her money every month, and she would have to make do with what she had. Yaya noticed how Jerrel talked about the other females that he was used to and how they all wanted money, but he just met her and was cashing out big time in the mall. That move right there said a lot about his character.

"Jerrel, are you sure that wasn't too much stuff?" Yaya asked as she watched him put her bags into his trunk.

"Girl, stop playing with me. It's your birthday and you deserve the best, right?"

Yaya sat back thinking about how much of a sucker he was for her pretty brown ass. She'd only known the nigga for a few days, and she already had him spending that bread on her. She knew that it would only be a matter of time before he started telling her all she needed to know about his family business.

"What you wanna do now?" He asked.

"I don't know. You're the one that wanted me to chill with you all day, maybe you should have planned the day a little better."

"Ok, smart ass. It would have been easier for me if you would have told me a little more about yourself. I need to know what you like to do and stuff like that, especially if you're gonna be my girl."

"Your girl? That's the role you're trying to get me to play?" Yaya teased with a smile on her face, so that he didn't get mad.

"Yeah, that's the role that I want you to play in my life, silly ass."

Without warning, Jerrel leaned over towards Yaya and slowly placed a kiss on her lips. This time, Yaya didn't push him away. Instead, she allowed his tongue to dance around in her mouth. She couldn't lie, he was good at what he did, and she was enjoying his touches even though she wasn't supposed to. He was making it hard for her not to enjoy the time she spent with him.

Finally, Yaya pushed away. "Ok, that's enough."

"Why? You can't tell me that you wasn't feeling it."

"I was, but I don't wanna rush things with us. Let shit happen naturally."

"Alright, I can fuck with that."

Jerrel drove off with a smile on his face. Never had a girl stopped him from getting what he wanted. At the same time, he liked her even more for not being so easy. Every man should have a challenge from time to time, and he had his right now.

"Damn, birthday girl, you were right."

"About what, Jerrel?"

"I do wish that I would have planned this day out better. To be honest, I just wanted to be around you, and now I'm just driving around lost as on what to do."

Jerrel tried to be real with her without telling her that by now, most girls would have been sucking his dick while he drove to the cheapest hotel. He didn't know how to entertain a girl without feeding them, spending a little bread and then fucking them. Yaya made him feel like he was an average ass nigga. but he still wanted her.

"I like normal things that most people like. Let's see, I love the zoo and different types of museums, the movies, and skating. It's the simple things that impress me the most."

Yaya leaned over to plate a kiss on Jerrel's check as he drove around. All the things that she named were things that she enjoyed doing before her life changed. Jerrel took in the information that she provided. In all honesty, he dug how regular she was and wanted to hang around her even more.

"Let me see what I can do, birthday girl."

Jerrel pulled into a gas station then pulled out his phone. Yaya didn't say much but watched as he jumped on the phone and looked up some stuff.

"Hey, you want something out of here?"

"Just a bottle of water would be fine. Thank you."

Jerrel liked how she said thank you for a bottle of water. He was loving how she acted. He could remember treating bitches to thousand-dollar clothes and shoes, then hundred-dollar meals, and at the end of the night, the bitch hadn't said not one thank you for shit. He now knew that he had been fucking with the wrong type of bitches his whole life. After filling up the tank, he took off driving.

"Now that I know some shit that you like to do, I got something planned for you."

With a smile on her face, Yaya sat back sipping on her water.

~

The two walked hand in hand, staring at the paintings on the wall.

"Oh my God. This one right here is beautiful, but you can tell that the artist was really in his feelings and depressed when he did this one. It looks like he painted it straight from his soul."

Jerrel looked at the painting again for a quick minute then back at her. "How can you tell all that just by looking at it?"

"Just look at the strokes of the brush. Nothings rushed, but he clearly took his time with each stroke. Then look at how sad the couple is in the picture. Nothing screams happiness looking at this. No happy colors just dark colors. Those are always a sign of depression."

Jerrel focused back on the painting. He tried to look at things how she was and still didn't understand.

Yaya let go of his hand. "Baby, look at this one. This is another one of his. You can look at this one and all the darkness in this one. He was clearly depressed and calling out for help thru his paintings."

Before Jerrel could respond, an older lady who was standing next to them jumped into their conversation. "You know, young lady, you're absolutely right. A few years after showing the world his amazing talent, he killed himself."

Yaya's mouth dropped wide. "Wow, I never knew that."

"You probably weren't even born when that happened, baby," the older lady said before walking off.

"Damn, baby, I guess you know your stuff. Brains and beauty, I like that."

"When I was younger, my mom was into art. I was her shadow, so I picked up some things," Yaya admitted.

Jerrel saw that her facial expression changed, and she now looked a little sad. "What's wrong?"

Yaya forced herself back into character. "Nothing. Come on, let's go over there."

Yaya took his hand again then lead him to the other side of the room. She had to remember to keep her cool at all times.

They looked at a few more paintings before they decided to leave. Jerrel helped Yaya into the car before going over to his side.

"That was my first time inside an art museum. Matter of fact, that was my first time in any museum period, but I had a good time. I never realized how much cool shit was in there."

"I haven't been there in years but enjoyed myself. Thank you for taking me."

Jerrel leaned over to steal a kiss.

"You stay tryna kiss on me," she jokingly teased.

"How could I not? You're so fucking beautiful and it feels so good when our lips connect."

Jerrel was so smooth with his words and constantly had Yaya blushing. She couldn't help but to fall for him. This time, she was the one leaning over kissing on him. Jerrel was ready for whatever and easily helped guide her onto his lap. The two hungrily attacked each other's lips as he palmed a handful of her ass. It wasn't until things got a little carried away and her ass hit the horn that they pulled away from each other. They both looked around to make sure they didn't have an audience. After seeing that no one was in the parking lot, they both started to laugh.

"Man, you got a nigga stuck, girl."

"Is that a good thing or bad thing?"

Jerrel took her hand then placed it on his hard dick.

"What you think?"

Yaya snatched her hand away then climbed back into the passenger seat.

Jerrel once again could see the change in her. "You good?"

"Yeah," Yaya mumbled.

Jerrel started the car then drove off. He wasn't sure where he was going, but he knew he needed to make her smile again. It was hard, but he had to remind himself that she wasn't like the rest and that her hand on his big hard dick wasn't gonna make her day.

Yaya sat there quietly. She was having a war within herself. She liked Jerrel and enjoyed the kiss. She liked the way his dick got hard for her, but she was trying not to let her feelings get in the way of what she needed to do. She was going back and forth in her head, wondering if she'll be wrong to have her cake and eat it too. Would it really be betrayal against her mom and brother if she enjoyed herself before the hurting? As he drove, she came to the conclusion that she can be happy with life as long as she got the job done. Besides, she needed him to be around in order to get to the main boss… Jackson.

Jerrel wanted to invite Yaya back to his house but decided to just drive her home. After parking in front of her house, he got out to help grab her bags.

"I got it, Jerrel," Yaya said, trying to pick everything up in one trip.

"Stop tripping and let me help you. You not about to carry all this shit in by yourself."

"Jerrel, I appreciate the offer, but please let me do it."

Jerrel raised his hands up, showing that he surrendered.

"Your grandma not gon' be tripping on you when she see you walk in with all them bags, is she? I mean, it's clear that you didn't get this shit from school."

"Did you forget that I'm 18 now? I'm grown and playing by my own rules."

"Ok, Ms. Grown Ass. I'm just gonna stick around to make sure you make it in alright."

Jerrel watched her carry in a few bags before she came out to get the rest. Before he closed the trunk, he pulled Yaya into a tight hug.

"I'm about to go up to this shop and check on shit. Hit me up once you get settled in."

"Alright. And thanks again for the birthday gifts and taking me to the museum."

"No problem, that was nothing. I did promise you a good time."

Jerrel gave Yaya a kiss before she walked back into the house with the rest of her bags.

Jerrel drove off thinking about how Yaya had his mind all fucked up. He couldn't believe that he spent most of the day with her and didn't even fuck. She was younger than him but was teaching him how to control himself. He was at the stage where settling down didn't sound like a bad idea after all.

"Where the hell you been, Yaya? The school called saying that you weren't in any of your classes today. Just because you're 18 now, don't get to smelling yourself."

"Grandma, chill out. I had other things to do. Besides, I'm grown now. Ain't no caseworker gon' be snooping around the house."

Grandma Jean wasted no time calling her out on her bullshit.

"I saw your fast tail out there with that grown man. I knew you were gonna be a young hoe just like your mama. She had a thing for older men too."

Grandma Jean started walking closer to Yaya. Yaya wasn't a fool and knew that if she didn't walk away, she was gonna be hit. She tried to take off, but her grandma hurried to grab the broom. Yaya let out a scream before making it up the steps. The broom handle bust her in the head.

"I already had to deal with your black ass, you bet not bring home any damn babies. I'll beat you both!" Grandma Jean yelled up the stairs.

In her bedroom, Yaya cried and paced the floor. That bullshit her grandma was on wasn't how she wanted to end her birthday at all. Then, to top shit off, her bags were still downstairs with her evil grandma. She could never understand how someone could be so evil.

~

"Where the hell you been, bro?" Jacques asked his big bro as he walked into the shop.

Jerrel took a seat in one of the chairs so that he could talk to his brother before he got some work done. "I had shit to take care of. Why, what's up?"

"Shit, nothing really. I just thought your ass would have been here before 4pm. Your ass ain't even been answering the phone, so now I'm wondering what the hell you been up to."

Jerrel grinned. "Yaya."

Jacques had a puzzled look on his face. "The chick from the boutique?"

"Yeah, that's exactly who I'm talking about. Today is her birthday and I took her out."

"So, that's the smile of getting new pussy?"

"Nah, it's nothing like that. We went to an art museum and grabbed something to eat."

Jacques laughed at his brother. "Art museum? Nigga, you bugging for real, dog. What the fuck y'all do at a fucking art museum?"

"We looked at art, you stupid muthafucka. It ain't always about pussy, lil bro."

"Then what the fuck is it about, nigga?" Jacques asked.

Jerrel stood back up from the chair. Just that fast, he was irritated by Jacque's ways. "Grow the fuck up, nigga," he said, walking back out of the shop. Whatever paperwork he had to do would just have to be done later.

Jacques chuckled as he watched his big brother leave.

"What's wrong with that nigga?" Their cousin Mike asked.

"He pussy whipped over a little bitch that he ain't even hit yet. That bitch got my brother wide the fuck open, and I don't like that shit."

Mike joined Jacques in laughter.

~

The sound of her phone going off woke Yaya straight out of her sleep.

"Damn," she said, rubbing her head.

Sitting up, she looked at the time on her phone and noticed that she had been sleep for a few hours. It was no surprise that it was Kiara texting her.

*Kiara: Hey birthday, girl, wyd?*

*Yaya: Hey, boo, just got back up. I swear I was just about to hit you up.*

*Kiara: What's good? When do you work next?*

*Yaya: Tomorrow*

*Kiara: Oh ok. Well, Rod's funeral is Saturday, I would really like it if you were there to support me.*

*Yaya: You're my best friend, you know you don't have to ask. I was already coming, boo.*

*Kiara: So, what's been going on with you? What did you do today?*

*Yaya: Now you know my granny don't do birthdays, but I went to an art museum and enjoyed myself*

*Kiara: With who 'cause you barely leave the house unless you're going to school?*

Yaya paused as she thought about if she should tell Kiara about Jerrel. After a short second, she decided to text her back.

*Yaya: Bestie, I swear if I told you the truth, you might not believe me.*

*Kiara: Who, bitch???? Spill the tea now.*

Yaya quickly texted back Jerrel's name. Kiara let out a light scream. She had wanted Jerrel for herself, but since her best friend pulled him, she was still happy.

*Kiara: Omg, bitch! Do you know how jealous hoes are gonna be of you? I'm so happy for you.*

Kiara really was happy for her friend although she wished that it was her.

*Yaya: Calm down, we're just friends. He's cool to talk to and hang around.*

The girls talked a little longer about Yaya's birthday. She wasn't a bit surprised when Kiara suggested that she should have fucked him to make sure she kept her place with him. She ended the conversation with simply telling her that she had other plans for him.

# Chapter 6

"Where are you going, Yaya?"

Yaya turned around to address her grandma. "I told you that Kiara's cousin's funeral was today."

"Oh damn, it is Saturday. I want you to come right home afterwards. I think it's time for these walls to be washed down again."

Yaya rolled her eyes. She had only been trying to keep her cool because she needed somewhere to stay until the state put her money into her account. She had already made the plans of leaving the same day her money hit.

"Yes, ma'am."

Yaya then walked to Kiara's house so she could get a ride to the funeral.

As the service went on, Yaya cried, but not one tear was for Rod. She thought back to her mom and brother's funeral. To everyone that was there, they thought she was crying and supporting her friend, but really, she was in her own little world. She hated to see folks standing in front of the church crying, saying that he was a good man, when he was a drug dealer that also killed for a muthafucka named Jackson.

The family and friends all gathered at a small hall after the service. Yaya was only worried about eating.

"Hey, boo, how are you holding up?"

Kiara took a seat at the table that Yaya had been sitting at. "To be honest, now that the funeral is over, I'm feeling much better."

"Ok, I'm glad to hear that."

The girls picked over their plates and talked a little more before a guy took a seat across from them.

"What's up, Kiara? How are you holding up, baby girl?"

"Hey, James. I'm good, and you? I know Rod was your best friend."

"I hurt like hell 'cause that was my nigga since day one. I can't believe he gone," James said.

"It'll be alright, we're gonna get thru this together," Kiara assured him.

All while Kiara was trying to comfort James, he kept eyeing Yaya.

"Hey, who's your friend? She sitting over there quiet as hell."

Kiara looked over to Yaya. "This is my bestie, boy."

"Does your bestie have a name?"

"She sitting right there, ask her," Kiara said, giggling.

James looked Yaya in her eyes. "What's your name, shorty?"

"Ayanna."

"Ayanna, that's a pretty name to fit such a beautiful woman like you. Look, I'm was about to head out, but can I get your number? I would love to call you sometimes."

Yaya gave him a strange look. "Don't you think it's the wrong time and place for this?"

Kiara laughed at her friend.

"My bad, shorty, you right. I'm gonna head on out." James gave Yaya one last look before leaving the table.

"Girl, you hurt that nigga's feelings," Kiara said, still laughing.

"Man, maybe I should go talk to him. I hate to make people feel bad."

Yaya got up from the table then went outside. She spotted James smoking a cigarette outside of his car.

"Hey, James, I hope I wasn't too mean in there."

"Nah, shorty, you good. I get it, you were trying to be supportive of your friend."

Yaya gave him a smile as she put her plan in motion. She walked closer towards him then gently rubbed his arm.

"You're so fucking pretty, girl," James admitted.

"Thank you. So, you still want my number?"

"Hell yeah, you know I do."

James handed Yaya his phone so that she could put her number in it. She wasn't sure what the plan was gonna be, but she needed to have him around for later.

Yaya put on an angry face as she took her seat back at the table.

"What's wrong with you?"

Looking Kiara straight in the face, Yaya played her role. "I thought we were friends, Kiara."

"We are, what are you talking about?"

"Look, it's not the right time or place for all this, but don't worry about me calling you anymore."

Kiara followed Yaya back out the door. "What's wrong, Yaya?"

"Every guy that comes around, you try to hook them up with me. I'm supposed to be your friend, not a hoe that you can past around."

"Yaya, I'm so sorry. I just wanted to see you happy with someone. I never wanted you to feel like I was trying to trick you out."

"I told you that I was talking to someone and you pretended to be happy when all along, you were really jealous. Just admit it, you wanted Jerrel for yourself and that's why you keep trying to hook me up with these old as men." Yaya's fake tears rolled down her face. "I gotta go."

Kiara watched as Yaya walked off. She wanted to chase after her, but she knew that Yaya was in her feelings and needed some space.

Yaya made it around the corner before fixing her face. She wasn't sure how she was gonna push Kiara out of her life, but Kiara playing matchmaker made things easier for Yaya. Yaya caught two buses home. While riding the bus, she put together a plan that could only go wrong if she fucked up.

Looking thru the pile of mail on the table, she saw an envelope with her name on it from the state, making her smile.

"Yes, my money is here," she mumbled.

"Little girl, what you doing going thru my mail?" Grandma Jean asked, walking out of the kitchen.

"Here goes your mail," Yaya said, handing over the rest of the envelopes, but stuffing hers in her purse.

"What was that? Was that the bank card?"

"Don't worry about it. Whatever it was, it had my name on it."

Yaya watched as her grandma reached for the broom. Instead of running, she stood there ready. In order for her plan to work, she needed to take a hit or two for the team. Grandma Jean snatched the broom up then quickly swung it at Yaya.

"Ungrateful, smart mouthed bitch. You gon' give me that card. That's my money!" She yelled.

Yaya took a hit to the face that damn near knocked her out before taking off running up the stairs. Once in her room and calming down, she pulled out her phone. She sent Jerrel a quick text.

*Yaya: Hey, I made it home from the funeral. Do you still wanna meet up tonight?*

Yaya sat the phone down as she examined her body in the full-size mirror on her wall. She knew her grandma too well and knew that she could get her to fall straight into her plan. Hearing her phone go off, she knew that Jerrel was texting her back.

*Jerrel: Hell yeah. Can I come get you now?*

*Yaya: How about I'll meet you at the shop in an hour?*

Jerrel texted back ok without asking any questions. He was just happy to see her again.

After a shower, Yaya got dressed. She wasn't sure if her grandma was in her room yet, but she needed to get out the house again. She slowly crept down the steps, hoping not to call any attention to herself. It was just her luck that Grandma Jean was tired and in her bed by now. Yaya snuck out the door without any problems. She then stood on her porch waiting on her Uber. She caught it to the store on the corner of the Barbershop. She needed to get into character. As she got to closer towards the shop, she started to cry. She then messed her hair up just a little. Yaya had a way of thinking about her mom or brother to make herself cry.

Jerrel had just pulled up when he saw her coming towards the shop. He quickly got out of the car.

"What's wrong, Yaya?" He asked as he wrapped her up into his arms.

Yaya kept crying but didn't say anything.

"Baby, tell me what's wrong."

"I can't tell you, I'm so scared," she cried out and made her body do a little shake.

"Look, come in the office and we can talk."

"No!" She yelled.

Jerrel looked Yaya over completely. He noticed the bruise on her face and her hair was out of place like she had been fighting. He then grabbed her, tossing her into his car.

"Who the fuck did this to you? Who hurt you? I swear to God, I will kill them."

Yaya cried a little harder to be a little more dramatic. "I didn't want you to go out your way to come get me, so I caught the bus here. While coming this way, this guy from my hood that's always trying to talk to me was bothering me like always. But this time was different. He had to be drunk or something 'cause he kept grabbing me, Jerrel."

Jerrel didn't let her finish before he started the car.

"Tell me where this nigga at. Where the fuck were y'all atwhen this happened?"

"Baby, slow down, you're scaring me!" She yelled out, noticing how he had started speeding.

Jerrel finally noticed that he was doing 80 going up 7 Mile. He then took his foot off the gas. He rubbed her leg as she sat there shaking in fear. "I'm sorry, baby. I'm pissed off and wanna hurt that nigga that hurt you so bad right now."

"I'll be ok. I'm just a little shaken up right now, but I feel safe now that I'm with you."

Jerrel stopped at the red light. He leaned over to give Yaya a kiss. "I hear you saying you good now, but I hate to see that bruise on your beautiful face."

Yaya put her head down as she thought of something else to say.

"I see that guy all the time and it's crazy how he really tried to rape me tonight. Maybe I shouldn't have been out so late. "

"Nah, baby, don't do that shit. Don't blame yourself for that bitch ass nigga's actions. I'm gonna kill that nigga."

Jerrel parked in front of a house that she didn't recognize.

"Aye, I need to do something right quick. You gon' be good for five minutes?"

"Yes, baby. Just make sure the doors are locked," she said, still playing her role.

Soon as Jerrel got out of the car, Yaya pulled out the phone that she had stolen from Kiara at the repast. She quickly texted James' phone.

*Yaya from Kiara's phone: Hey, James, I'm texting you for Yaya. Her peoples real mean and might trip on you since you're a little older, so please delete all messages after you read them. My girl said you been on her mind since the funeral today. She said can y'all meet at the park in the hood. She really wanna see you.*

James, not knowing any better, quickly texted her back.

*James: Ok cool. I'll erase the shit, but tell her yeah, just text me when.*

*Yaya from Kiara's phone: Ok, just wait on her to text you. She about to get dressed.*

Yaya tossed the phone into her purse as Jerrel climbed back in the car.

"See, I told you that wouldn't be long. I just had to handle something for my dad right quick, but I'm all yours for the night."

"To be honest, I'm just so tired and my body is hurting so bad from fighting that nigga off me."

Jerrel wanted her to chill with him for the night, but he wasn't sure if he should bring it up since she had just got attacked. Trying to be a gentleman he messaged her thigh, just enough to keep her calm.

"You want me to take you home so you can relax your body and get some rest?"

"My grandma is gone and I really don't wanna be by myself tonight. I think I'm more shaken up then I been telling you."

Jerrel now had a smirk on his face. "Don't worry, I got you, ma."

Jerrel had done something that he had never done before. He allowed a chick outside of family to come to the house that he shared with his brother. They always had a rule to never really have company there because they never knew what a person's real attentions were. He trusted that Yaya wasn't gonna be a threat.

As they walked in, Yaya looked around and was instantly impressed. "This a nice place. You live here by yourself?"

"Nah. When I brought this crib, my baby brother moved in with me. He delivered y'all food before. You remember Jacques?"

"Oh, yeah, I do remember him."

"You want something to eat or drink?"

"Some water would be nice."

Jerrel took her by the hand before taking her upstairs to his room. "Look, get comfortable and I'm gonna go get your water."

Jerrel never dealt with a girl that only drank water. Most bitches would have been screaming out Hennessy or something. What he didn't know was that she had only been drinking water since she started living with her granny. She got used to only having it. He grabbed a bottle of water out the fridge then snuck back up the stairs. He was praying that he didn't catch her doing anything sneaky and was surprised to see her staring in the mirror crying. He slowly walked up behind her then wrapped his arms around her waist.

"It's gonna be alright baby."

"Look at my face, he fucked up my face," she cried.

"It's gonna be ok, I'm gonna handle that nigga for you. What's his name again?"

"His name is James, he's older than us."

Hearing that really pissed him off. Not only did the nigga attack her and leave a bruise, but he was an old, washed up ass nigga. Although Jerrel had just met Yaya, he felt like it was only right to make her feel better. After wiping away her tears, he gave her the bottle of water. Yaya sipped on her water as she watched him dig in his drawer, pulling out a t-shirt.

"Here, you can go right thru those doors and take a hot bath so you can relax your body. Afterwards, you can take the bed. I'm not trying to rush shit, so I'll sleep on the couch if that'll make you feel better."

Yaya smiled. "Thank you, Jerrel. I swear you so sweet."

Once Yaya was in the tub, Jerrel stepped in. "Aye, I have a question. Where the fuck that nigga be at?"

"Huh?

"Where that nigga be at that attacked you?"

"At that park, not too far from my house. I think he be up there selling drugs."

Jerrel had a strange look on his face. From his knowledge none of his dad's workers did any work at the hood parks where kids be hanging at. So, not only was the man a pervert ass rapist, but he was trying to step on his dad's toes. He really needed to die.

Yaya climbed out the tub and wrapped the towel that Jerrel had left for her around herself. She needed to, so that she could hear what Jerrel was on the phone talking about.

"Yeah, we're gonna have to take that nigga out, tonight. He crossed too many lines and you know I don't play that shit," Jerrel said over the phone.

Hearing Yaya walking into the room, Jerrel turned around to get a peek at her. Although she was wrapped up in her towel, Jerrel had a little smirk on his face. He couldn't help but to react to the sight of her.

"Damn."

Knowing exactly what she was doing to him, she grinned before dropping her towel then putting on the T-shirt that he have given her.

"Aye, I need that handled tonight. I might be a little tied up. Just hit me up once it's done."

Jerrel ended his phone call then walked over towards Yaya. He then pulled her into a hug.

"How are you feeling now?"

"To be honest, I'm actually feeling good in your arms."

Jerrel could feel his dick getting hard and didn't want to scare her off. He gave her a kiss then pulled away. Yaya wasn't stupid and knew what was going on. She had to decide if she wanted Jerrel as bad as her body was screaming out for him. Yaya had never really given herself to anyone, but her grandma's brother always thought that she was his personal fuck buddy for a year straight.

"Do you feel comfortable here with me?"

Yaya hesitated answering for a minute. " I feel comfortable here, but I'm nervous a little."

Jerrel took her hand. "Look, I told you that I want you for real, and I'm not trying to rush you to do anything. Like I said before, I'll give you the bed, and I'll talk the couch."

To his surprise, Yaya led his hand under her shirt.

"I'm not nervous about being here with you. I was nervousabout how I was gonna tell you that I wanted you just as bad as you wanted me."

Hearing that had Jerrel grinning like a kid on Christmas. He wanted her so bad and didn't wanna waste any time. He quickly removed his shirt while kicking off his shoes. Yaya wasn't sure what to do with herself, so she let him take control. Jerrel stood face to face with her. He had only his boxers on but took no time snatching her shirt off.

"Damn, baby, you're so fucking sexy," he said, lifting her up and placing kisses all over her.

Yaya let out a moan. She was loving the way he was making her body feel. After her grandma's brother died years ago, she always wondered how her real first time would be and who it would be with. Never in her life did she imagine sleeping with a guy that she'd only known for a week. Some might judge her, but she deserved to be happy for once.

Jerrel took his time with her. She was shaking so bad, he knew that she was scared and assumed that she must have never been with anyone. Placing her on the edge of the bed, Jerrel leaned down just enough to give her one last kiss before laying her completely down. He then kissed his way down to her breasts where he took his time going back and forth placing each into his mouth. For some reason, he had always been a titty man.

"This sweet chocolate melting in my mouth," he whispered before sliding his tongue down her stomach.

Yaya had a hard time not thinking about the head that she got from Rod the night that she killed him when Jerrel placed her pussy in his mouth.

"Damn," he whispered as he used his tongue to please her.

Yaya was fighting her feelings. She wanted to moan out in pleasure, but her hands were busy pushing his head away.

"Come on, baby, don't do that."

Trying her best stop fighting him, Yaya became vocal. "Oh my God, Jerrel, that shit feels so good. Please don't stop, baby."

"I got you, baby."

Soon, Yaya hound herself cuming like crazy and Jerrel happily enjoyed every ounce of fluid that squirted out of her. He used his t-shirt to wipe his face once he was ready to really get down to business. Yaya scooted back towards the middle of the bed.

"Man, where the hell you going?"

In such a shy, sweet voice, Yaya answered, "It's too wet right there."

Jerrel couldn't help but to laugh.

"You so fucking silly."

Jerrel quickly got serious as he climbed on top of Yaya. Her body shook, but he took his time entering her.

"Jerrel…" she moaned out, feeling his head slowly opening her up.

"I got you, baby," he whispered as he pushed his way into her and kissed on her.

Jerrel could feel the grip that her walls had on his dick. He wanted so badly to give her a good pounding, but the tears in her eyes told him to continue to give her slow, passionate strokes. Yaya was everything and more that he had imagined. He couldn't believe how her young ass had him cumming a little after fifteen minutes. She was definitely working with something. Afterwards, Jerrel held her closely in his arms and occasionally placed soft kisses on her.

"You alright? I swear I tried to be gentle with you."

Yaya turned around to face him. "I'm alright, Jerrel. I know you tried."

Yaya rested her head on his chest. Although she was hurting, she also felt good and loved all in one. She was happy that he didn't bring up the fact that she cried a little. When he asked if she wanted him to stop, she told him no. Truthfully, she didn't wanna seem like a big baby and scare him off. She wanted Jerrel all to herself.

After going another round, Yaya and Jerrel cuddled up and drifted off to sleep. Not even a good twenty minutes later, Jerrel's phone started to go off. He ignored the first call, but the second call, he answered.

"What's good, my nigga? How that shit turn out?"

Yaya woke up once she felt Jerrel get out the bed. Instead of saying anything, she pretended to still be sleep, so that she could hear what he was talking about.

"Ok, cool, my nigga. Look, I'm gonna holler at you on the morning with your bread," Jerrel said into his phone before placing it back down on the dresser.

After climbing back into the bed, he pulled Yaya into his arms then placed a kiss on her neck.

"I got that nigga handled for you. You ain't never got to worry about him trying to hurt you again."

Jerrel gave her one last kiss before closing his eyes and drifting off.

# Chapter 7:

"Damn, what you doing, bro, you just moved ole girl in? What happened to us not letting hoes know where the crib at?" Jacques asked while talking a seat at the kitchen island.

For the last month or so, Jerrel and Yaya had been boo'ed up like an old married couple. Although Jacques didn't care too much for Yaya, he still tried his hardest not to disrespect her, especially in front of his brother. The thing was, when they got that place, they both agreed not to have random ass hoes running in and out the crib. Yet, Jerrel's sucker for love ass had just moved a chick in without even talking to his baby brother.

"First of all, bro, Yaya not no fucking hoe, so don't come down here starting that shit. I'm trying to make breakfast, not hear your mouth."

Before Jacques could respond, Yaya walked into the kitchen. "Good morning, everyone."

"Morning," Jacques coldly said before grabbing an apple from the fruit bowl then walking out of the kitchen.

Jerrel didn't pay him attention as he walked over to Yaya and gave her a kiss.

"Good morning, baby. How did you sleep?"

"Now you know I sleep so good in your arms. I only woke up because I didn't feel you anymore."

"Why don't you take a seat so you can get some food in you?

Yaya took a seat at the island while Jerrel made her plate. "Baby, I was thinking that maybe I should go home. I don't want to make your brother feel uncomfortable."

Jerrel took a seat across from Yaya with their plates. "That nigga alright, ma, you ain't gotta go nowhere. I'll talk to him about acting crazy."

Yaya smiled knowing that he was on her side. It was just a matter of time before they would be completely beefed out. As she ate her breakfast, she thought about what her next move was gonna be.

"Jacques, Jacques! Aye, bro, you gon' come eat?" Jerrel called out.

It took a minute for Jacques to walk back into the kitchen. He didn't say anything to them as he fixed his plate. He loves that his brother seemed happy, but something deep in his spirit didn't feel right with Yaya. To him, she played that sweet, innocent, shy role, but he could feel something off with her. His brother wasn't tryna hear that shit, so he took it upon himself to watch her ass.

After breakfast, Yaya washed the dishes before returning to Jerrel's bedroom. She didn't have to work that Saturday and wanted to see what he had planned for them.

"I know you happy next week is your graduation, baby."

"Yes, my graduation is next weekend, and I couldn't be happier."

"Have you thought about what you wanna do afterwards?"

Yaya stepped out of the walk-in closet that she now shared with Jerrel. "To be honest, I haven't decided yet. A part of me wanna go to college and study art, but a part of me wanna travel the world. Sad to say, but I never been out of Detroit."

"Damn, baby, it looks like I'm going have to change that and book some flights. Trust me, once you leave Detroit, you might not wanna come back," Jerrel said, thinking about where he could take her after her graduation. Their relationship developed overnight, but from what he could tell, they were truly happy with each other.

"I have a surprise for you, Yaya," Jerrel announced as they climbed out of the shower.

"What is it? I swear you be spoiling me."

Wrapped up in a towel, Jerrel took a seat on the edge of the bed before motioning for her to take a seat too.

"Every month, my family has this big dinner just to play catch up with one another and tonight, you'll be able to meet my whole family."

"Oh, wow! Are you serious? You must really like me."

"Yeah, I do, but what was all that for?" He asked, feeling like she was trying to start some mess.

Yaya stood up from the bed. "Nothing, Jerrel, don't worry about it."

Jerrel jumped up from the bed, grabbing her by the arm. "Don't walk away from me, Yaya. What's up?"

Yaya looked down at the floor. "Nothing, baby, just forget about it."

"Fuck that shit, what's the fucking problem?" He asked again.

"I guess it got around my school that we were messing around and bitches started talking about how you and your brother were known for fucking bitches then leaving them. So, it just surprised me that you want me to meet the rest of your family."

Jerrel stood there staring Yaya in her pretty brown eyes. He didn't wanna lie to her because what those bitches said was true, but at the same time, he didn't wanna hurt her with the truth.

"Look, you should know that I really wanna be with you. Shid, I haven't showed you anything different. Whatever I did in the past is just that, the fucking past. Stop letting them jealous bitches put shit in your ears."

"I just don't wanna be sitting around growing feelings just to look stupid in the end, Jerrel," Yaya calmly said.

Jerrel pulled her into a hug. "I'll never have you out here looking stupid. Those jealous bitches just mad 'cause I'm not with their ass, and I treat you like the queen that you are."

Yaya did a complete circle in the tight-fitted red dress that Jerrel had bought for her to wear.

"How do I look, baby?"

"Damn, you look amazing. We might have to say fuck tonight and stay in."

That was the last thing that Yaya wanted. Tonight, was gonna be the night that she met Jackson.

"No, baby, this night is important to me."

"It is?" Jerrel questioned.

"Yes, baby. We've been together for a minute now, and I would love to meet your whole family."

"Oh, ok, I see."

Jerrel stood up from the bed then walked over towards Yaya. They both stood in front of the full body mirror admiring just how beautiful each other were.

"I don't want you to be nervous. You're such a sweet person, I know their gonna love you," he said, placing a kiss on her neck.

A warm feeling came over Yaya's body. She never meant to fall for him the way that she did, but it happened. Spending years of not being loved had fucked up her mental, and she felt like it was impossible for someone like her to be loved. It wasn't until she allowed Jerrel to love on her in the right way that she realized it was possible to be loved again. Jerrel let his hands roam all over Yaya's ass while he kissed on her neck.

"Come on, baby, let's not get into this. Let's go to this dinner, then when we come back here, you can have me for the rest of the night."

"Ok, baby, that sounds like a plan."

Yaya continued to fix her hair and makeup while Jerrel watched. Yaya couldn't help but to cheese at the sight of her man looking like a male model straight out of a GQ magazine.

"Damn, you so fucking sexy, Jerrel."

"I'm matching your fly, girl," he said with a grin on his face.

They both were looking good, and they couldn't keep their hands off each other.

"Come on, baby, you gon' fuck up my makeup. I told you, after dinner, I'll be all yours."

"Look at him, Yaya. I can't leave the house like this," he said, placing her hand over his hard penis.

"You lucky I love what you got to offer," she said, dropping to her knees.

Jerrel enjoyed the warmth of her mouth around his dick. He couldn't lie or pretend that she didn't know what she was doing. Before cumming, Jerrel pulled Yaya up then turned her around. He bent her down on the dresser, ready to give her some hard strokes. Pulling her dress up, he quickly slid her lace thong to the side so he could enter her.

"Damn, baby," Yaya moaned out, feeling every inch of his dick pushed in her.

Jerrel continued to give her deep stokes as his phone started to go off.

"Baby, your phone is going off."

"Fuck that phone, girl."

~

"Wow, this place is amazing," Yaya said, looking over the baby mansion where Jackson and his wife, Justice, lived.

"Yeah, once I settle down and get ready to have my own family, I'm gonna get me a dope ass spot like this for me and my girl."

"Oh really, is that right, Jerrel?"

Jerrel had a wide grin on his face, showing off his pretty white teeth. "Hell yeah, girl. Me and the right one won't be stuck in the hood forever. I got big plans and staying in Detroit ain't in my future."

"Oh, should I be worried?"

"Umm, let me think about that," he teased.

Feeling confused and unsure of her place in his life, Yaya's smile disappeared. Jerrel then pulled Yaya into a hug, so that he could whisper in her ear.

"You don't have shit to worry about. You got me, little mama."

"Who is this lovely young lady?"

Jerrel turned around to see his father standing there. "Hey, pops. This is my lil' lady Yaya. I talked to you about her before."

"Yaya, nice to finally meet you. I've heard so much about you, but now I can match a face with your name," Jackson said with lots of happiness in his voice.

Lately, whenever he spoke to his son, Jerrel was always taking about his favorite girl Yaya. He knew his son was in love with the pretty young lady that stood in his face. Jackson held his hand out for Yaya to shake, but she froze for a second. For years, she wondered who the big boss by the name of Jackson was, and now here he was standing in her face, pretending to be a good guy.

"Baby, you alright?"

Yaya quickly got back into character. "Yes, everything is fine. I'm sorry about that," she said, shaking Jackson's hand.

"Jerrel, go introduce her to the family. Let me go see if your mom is done getting ready. I'll talk to you later."

Jackson gave them one last look before walking off.

Jerrel took Yaya by the hand. "Baby, you don't have to be nervous around my family."

Still in character, Yaya responded, "I just never did all this before. I hope I'm not embarrassing you tonight.

"Hell nah, girl. If you feel uncomfortable, we can leave and go back to the crib."

"No, baby, that's not necessary. I'll be fine, I just need to warm up to everyone."

Jerrel made sure to introduce his lil lady to whoever was at the gathering. His family was happy that he had finally settled down. Everyone welcomed her with open arms except Jacques and one of their petty acting aunties. For some reason, Jacques liked when his brother was out tagging all the hoes with him. It had never been nothing personal about Yaya, he really just missed his brother. As far as their Auntie Janet, she was just petty and didn't give a fuck what came out her mouth.

As they sat around the dinner table, Yaya started to feel sick to her stomach. Just knowing that she was eating with the family that was responsible for her family's death didn't sit right with her at all.

"So, Yaya, how did you met my nephew?" Auntie Janet asked.

"I met him when I first started working at Glamour Girls."

His auntie gave her a strange look. "Seeing how Jerrel was raised, things must not be that serious yet because the women in our family don't work. We're all taken care of, and quite well at that."

Her outburst silenced the whole room and had everyone looking at Yaya and Jerrel. Most were low-key thinking it or wondered who she was, but only Janet had the balls to say anything. She had always been known for speaking her mind.

"Boy, I know you didn't bring one of your jump-offs to the family dinner."

"Auntie, with all respect, Yaya and I are happy with how things are between us. She's working until graduation, and that was her choice. Now can you mind your business?"

Janet continued to eat on her food, thinking of what to say next. She usually was quick on her feet with come backs, but this time, she was stuck.

Jerrel looked over towards Yaya. "You good?"

Yaya gave him a fake smile. "Yeah, I'm ok."

Jerrel gave her a small kiss to let her know that he had her back. Jacques sat across from his brother with the biggest smirk on his face.

"Damn, Auntie, you a fool for that one."

Jerrel gave his baby brother a strange look. He honestly was getting tired of his shit too.

"Aye, bro, I don't think you wanna fuck with me right now."

"Nigga, you not scaring shit. Fuck you, pussy whipped ass nigga!" Jacques yelled, jumping up from the table.

Just as things were about to pop off and everyone was arguing over who needed to be quiet, Jackson, who sat at the front of the table, stood up. Clearing his throat, the family all sat back down and remained quiet so he could speak. Yaya was amazed at how he had them all under control.

"Y'all know I don't play this shit. Since forever, it's always been family over everything and everybody.

All this arguing and shit at the dinner table…" Jackson paused on his speech. "I built this family up from selling drugs and now y'all acting wild like y'all hooked on the shit. This shit here is unacceptable."

"I apologize for fucking up dinner, little brother," Janet said, biting into her piece of steak.

"You damn near 50 years old, don't you think it's time to get your shit together? Or did you plan to be petty our whole life?"

Janet looked around as everyone laughed at her.

"Ok, Mr. Action Jackson. You ain't gotta put me on blast like that."

Jackson walked over towards Jerrel and Yaya.

"How do you think they felt? You don't know this young lady or how my son feels about her, and your big mouth was just a going. You need to apologize to them so we cancontinue our meal."

"I'm not a fucking kid, so I don't know who you think you're talking to right now. I don't apologize for shit."

Everyone's attention was on Janet now. Nobody never talked shit to Jackson and didn't have to deal with major consequences. Without saying a word, Jackson pulled Janet from her seat and dragged her away from the table. He had always been big on family and respect. A good ten minutes passed before Jackson and Janet walked back into the room.

"Jerrel, I would like to apologize to you and your date. I was out of line."

Jerrel nodded his head but didn't say anything. He really was over her childish behavior and didn't care to hear shit else from her.

After dinner, the family went into the party room. There were drinks and music playing for their entertainment.

"Baby, I'll be right back."

Jerrel refused to let her go. "Where you going?"

Yaya leaned in closer so that she could whisper. "Jerrel, I have to you pee, this wine is running thru me."

Jerrel released her arm. "You do know where the closest one is, don't you?"

"Yes, baby, Jewel showed me earlier."

"So, what's the beef with you and your brother?" Justice asked, walking up behind her son.

"He's mad because I'm done with all that bullshit chasing behind these bitches. I think I finally found the one and I'm happy for once," he admitted.

"I don't care how grown you think you are, don't sit in my face and call another female out her name."

"My bad, ma. Jacques just pissed me off feeding into Auntie's petty ass. I swear that lady loves creating drama."

Justice smiled at her son. "So, my oldest is finally in love, huh? I hope that means grandbabies, and lots of them."

Jerrel blushed. "I'm not saying all that, but she's special to me, ma. I mean, I've never felt this way before about no chick."

Jacques, who had been listening, jumped into their conversation. "That's because you a fucking sucker ass nigga."

Before Jerrel could respond, Justice went off.

"Maybe you need to learn from your brother and grow the fuck up. I been told y'all that it wasn't cool to play with people feelings. You still think it's cute to run around fucking these girls then leaving them? Just watch little nasty ass, your dick is gonna fall off."

Without waiting for Jacques to respond, Justice walked off. Jerrel walked past his brother, making sure to bump him hard enough to spill a little of his drink on his shirt.

"Bitch ass nigga," Jerrel mumbled as he went to look for Yaya.

Finishing up in the restroom, Yaya ended up getting a little lost looking at all the paintings on the wall. She wished that she knew they were there earlier 'cause she would have skipped dinner.

"What you doing, baby?" Jerrel asked, sneaking up on her.

She turned around with a huge smile on her face.

"Oh my God, baby, why didn't you tell me that all of this was up here?"

Jerrel didn't say anything but kept a smile on his face. It was something about seeing her so excited that made him happy.

"Baby, look at this painting right here. Isn't it beautiful?"

Jerrel had seen that painting for years and never paid it any mind until that evening.

"Yes, Bae, it's beautiful just like you."

Yaya blushed.

"Let's get back to this family shit," he said, grabbing hold to her hand.

Yaya felt a little better after Jackson stood up for her, but she wanted to get even with him on her own.

"You know, young lady, my ass don't really be meaning no harm. I just talk a little too much at the wrong time."

"It's ok. Let me go get you a drink from over there."

Janet didn't hesitate to show how much she wanted the drink. "Well, go ahead and get auntie a drink."

Yaya started to walk towards the bar. While walking around upstairs, she remembered that she had talked a guy named Fred who give her a vial of liquid date rape drug. She heard that he had some and had used it on two of their classmates. Using the information that she had, he was happy to hand it over to her. Just that fast, she came up with a plan to make big mouth Auntie Janet drink that shit right on up.

Janet took a big sip from her cup. "Damn, girl, I done apologized a few times, you ain't got to try to poison me. That shit was strong."

"My bad," Yaya said before walking off to be back with Jerrel.

Once Yaya reached Jerrel, he quickly questioned her. "Hey, baby, my auntie not still fucking with you, is she?"

"Oh no, she actually apologized again and now she seems nice."

Jerrel laughed. "Don't let that liquor fool you. She still be doing too much."

"Enough of that, let's dance. You know this my song."

Jerrel took Yaya to the dance floor so that they could dance the night away.

**Across The Room**

"Auntie, let me get a sip," Jewel said, holding her hand out.

"Girl, now you know your daddy will kill my ass. I'm buzzing not drunk out my damn mind. Besides, I think I pissed him off enough tonight."

"Auntie, I won't tell him. Please," Jewel begged.

Tired of hearing her niece begging and loving to go against Jackson, Janet passed her the cup. "Drink slowly and not a lot, little girl."

Jewel took the cup out her hand then took a big gulp. "Damn, that shit was strong."

Janet snatched her cup. "Hardheaded ass little girl."

All while this was going on, Yaya watched as they passed the cup back and forth, drinking on her special drink. Although the drink wasn't meant for Jewel, Yaya smiled knowing that the family was about to feel her pain.

"Somebody get some help!" Janet yelled.

Turning around, Jerrel and Yaya could see Jewel lying on the floor.

"What the fuck!" Jerrel yelled as he ran over towards his sister. Playing her part, Yaya was right behind him.

"Somebody call the ambulance!" Jackson yelled.

Everyone crowded around Jewel as she laid out on the floor.

"What the fuck happened, Janet?" Jackson yelled.

Janet stood there not feeling too well herself. With a fainted voice, Janet told them that she didn't know what happened to her. She lied, fearing that Jackson was gonna attack her.

Justice made her way through the crowd. "What happened to my baby?" She cried out, walking in Janet's face.

Janet was felt lost as she tried to talk to her family.

"I don't feel right," she mumbled.

No one really paid her any attention as they tried to wake Jewel up. That was until she fell out next to Jewel.

"Oh my God, what's going on?" Yaya yelled out.

Yaya pretended to be just as concerned as the family. She had fake tears rolling down her face and begged Jewel and Janet to wake up.

~

"Baby, come sit down and try to relax. I promise you the doctors are doing everything in their power to help your sister and auntie."

Jerrel paced the floors while waiting to hear what was going on with his people. Jackson held on to Justice, promising her that everything was gonna be alright. He had always been a street nigga and never let anything scare him but that night, he was scared and actually could feel himself on the verge of crying.

Yaya walked in front of Jerrel to stop him from walking. "It's gonna be ok, love," she said, giving him a hug.

Jacques sat the across the small waiting room in his feelings about his family and hating the sight of Jerrel hugging on Yaya like that night was about her ass. Wasn't shit going on that night her concern. She needed to leave and let the family work out their personal business.

"Aye, bro, this a family thing. Don't you think your girl should go home and check on her own family?"

"Right now ain't the right time or place for your bullshit, bro. Just stay your ass over there and shut the fuck up," Jerrel responded.

"I'm just saying, why the fuck is she here, nigga?"

Jerrel released Yaya then tried to charge after Jacques. "I'll give you that ass whooping your bitch ass been begging for."

Jackson was tired of his sons' shit and with everything going on with his daughter and sister, he still managed to separate them.

"This bullshit has got to stop now. I don't know what the fucking problem is between y'all, but while we're here with my baby in their fighting for her life, I don't wanna hear shit!" He yelled.

Yaya picked her purse up from the chair and began to walk off. Just like she knew, Jerrel cane running after her.

"Come on, baby, don't pay that jealous nigga no attention. You have the right to be here with us."

Yaya stopped walking to talk to Jerrel. "Look, maybe I should just go home so that I won't be causing problems between you and your brother. I'm gonna just go to my granny's and chill for a while."

Yaya tried to walk away, but Jerrel grabbed her.

"Baby, you just don't know how scared I am right now. Ijust need you to be here with me. Please," he begged.

Yaya snatched her hand away. "Just call me and let me know what's going on with Jewel."

Just like that, Yaya walked away, leaving Jerrel stuck in his feelings. As bad as she hated it, she was about to go back to her granny's house. Yaya planned on using this time to get her thoughts together. Over time, she had caught real life feelings for Jerrel and actually liked being around his family, except Jacques. As bad as she wanted revenge, sometimes she just wanted to continue to be loved by Jerrel.

Yaya was surprised to see that her grandma was still up in the front room watching TV.

"What the hell are you doing here? What happened that little nigga you ran off with? Done spent all your fucking money? So now your black ass back here looking for three meals and somewhere to rest your head? You always been a bipolar, crazy, black bitch."

Yaya looked confused. How the hell did she forget that she had an account full of money? She was so used to

Jerrel spoiling her, she forgot that she had her own. Instead of wasting her time arguing with her grandma, she simply walked upstairs to grab some clothes that she had left, then went back out the door. Yaya knew that as bad as she wanted to be grown and on her own, she still had a lot of growing up to do.

"Fuck," she mumbled.

She pulled out her phone to see if she could find a hotel or something to stay at for the night. Times like this, she wanted to say fuck getting revenge on Jackson and go crawling back to Jerrel. She knew he would accept her back with open arms. After sitting around, Yaya finally was in her Uber and on her way downtown to the place that she planned on calling her own for a night or two.

After a hot shower, Yaya laid across the bed wishing she was in Jerrel's arms. She was so used to him that it was hard to sleep without him now. It took forever, but Yaya had finally doze off. She was pissed when her phone started to go off, waking her up.

"Yes, Jerrel?"

"Baby?"

Yaya set up. She could tell that he had been crying and drinking and was probably drunk, which wasn't a good sign.

"What's up, Jerrel, I was sleep."

"She's gone, baby. My sister is gone!" He cried.

"What? Oh my God, baby, I'm so sorry to hear that. Where are you?"

"Man, I was driving around drinking. This shit got me fucked up, ma."

"I know, baby. What happened?"

Jerrel didn't answer. All he could do was cry.

"Why did this happen to her, man? She was just a baby that didn't do shit to nobody," he cried.

"Baby, I know you're hurting, but I don't need you to be out drinking and driving. I can't have nothing happening to you."

Jerrel understood her completely. "Where you at, Yaya? I need you, baby. I need you so bad right now."

Yaya held the phone, telling him to go home and that she would catch an Uber to his place because she didn't want him driving around drunk. But he begged her to tell him where she was at. After he explained that he had went to her granny's house and got cussed out, Yaya told him exactly where she was staying. Jerrel promised to be there in no time. For some reason, he didn't wanna go to the house knowing that Jacques was gonna be there.

Yaya patiently waited for Jerrel to arrive. Deep down inside, she felt so bad for Jewel because they had actually become good friends. Jewel had always called her big sister.

Twenty minutes later, Jerrel called Yaya to let her know that he was downstairs. After getting him to the room, Yaya hugged on him as he cried in her arms. She knew that same hurt of losing a sibling. As she laid in the bed, he cried on her like a big baby and before she knew it, she was crying with him. Those tears really made her feel bad. All this time she had been calling everyone a monster, but she had become one herself.

That night, Yaya realized that she didn't want to live her life getting revenge. She wasn't sure if it was because of the way Jerrel cried to her that night, or how they made sweet love to one another. She couldn't stand to see him so broken. She was ready to spend the rest of her life wrapped up in his arms.

"Yaya, you sleep, baby?"

"Halfway, why, what's up, Jerrel? You need to talk or something?"

"Yeah, baby, I do," he admitted,

Yaya hugged him a little tighter. "I'm here for you."

"I haven't lost nobody since my grandma died when I was younger. Jewel really fucked me up with this shit, man. Then Auntie Janet fighting for her life right now. I never felt this weak before, man."

Yaya held on to him. She didn't know what to say. When her mom and brother died, everyone told her to keep her head up, or they told her that things were going get better in time. But now, 8 years later, she still cried her eyes out over her loved ones.

"I understand, baby. Trust me, I do. I just want you to know that I'm here for you no matter what. What did the doctors say happened because they were just fine? I mean, we were all just having a good time."

"They say it's looking like it was alcohol poison. My baby didn't even drink for real. I caught her stealing sips from time to time, but that was it. Man, this shit is crazy, Yaya."

Silence filled the room for a minute before Jerrel continued to talk. "Anyways, once her funeral is over, I want us to get a place."

Yaya was caught off guard. "What?"

"It's time for me to get a new crib without Jacques. I just want it to be us."

"But that's your brother, baby."

"Yeah, I kind of know that. I just think it's time to really be a man, and I want you there every step of the way."

There was no way that Yaya could ever think about walking away from him now. Jerrel never said anything, but she knew that they shared the same feelings deep inside.

Jerrel placed a kiss on Yaya. "I don't know what it is about you that makes me feel like this, but I'm happy as hell with you, and I love you."

"I love you too, baby."

Before going back to sleep, the couple made love again.

# Chapter 8

Although they had just buried their daughter that Monday, Justice and Jackson showed up to Yaya's graduation to support her. Jerrel was happy that they came, but he wasn't surprised at the fact that his brother didn't come. Yaya felt funny seeing them in the audience, knowing that if it wasn't for Jackson, her brother and mother would have been there to support her, but she kept her cool.

"Ayanna Fisher."

Hearing her name being called out and seeing Jerrel cheer for her had been the highlight of her day. As she walked across the stage, she cried. The feeling of accomplishing one of her goals was such a great feeling. After her graduation was over, Yaya stood around talking to a few of her classmates. They all were emotional not knowing if they were gonna see each other ever again. Just as Yaya was about to make her way to Jerrel, she was stopped by Kiara. They hadn't talked since her cousin's funeral, and truth be told, Yaya didn't wanna be bothered with her.

"Yaya, can we please talk?" Kiara asked.

"What can I help you with?" Yaya boldly asked.

Kiara could tell that she had an attitude, but she was ready to speak her mind. "Look, Yaya. I know shit went left with our friendship, but I think you took things too far. I even went to your grandma's house, and she was saying that you ran off. What did I do so bad that you would have her lying for you?”

“She wasn’t lying. I haven’t been home, but I don’t have to check in with you, girl.”

Kiara heard that Yaya had been staying with Jerrel, she just wanted to hear it out of Yaya’s mouth.

“Come on, Yaya, stop trying to make a problem by getting smart with me. I’m trying to be the bigger person and make this friendship work.”

“Just stop then. Don’t you understand that sometimes people out grow each other?”

Kiara stepped back. “Oh really? Well if that’s how you feel, I’m just gonna get moving.” Kiara started to walk off but quickly turned around. “You know what I find crazy?”

“What?”

“They found James dead.”

Yaya tried not to show her poker face. “Ok, and? He did live a wild lifestyle, anything could have happened to him.”

“I’m just saying, Rod was found dead after he met you and then James. What a fucking coincidence, ain’t it?”

Yaya started laughing. “I guess, girl. And it’s crazy that they both were cool with your ass too. Bitch, stop trying to connect them muthafuckas with me.”

Just like that, Yaya walked away. She didn’t have time for all that bullshit Kiara was talking about. Besides, she didn't want Jerrel to walk over there and hear that bullshit she was saying.

"Aye, baby, what's going on?"

Yaya pulled Jerrel away. "Nothing. I guess that's one of your fans and she tryna start some shit."

Before they could get too far, Kiara yelled out, "I saw the messages. I know what you did!"

Yaya continued to walk away knowing that her plan to just get away wasn't gonna be as easy as she thought. Kiara followed Yaya and Jerrel out of the door. Yaya was scared of Kiara saying anything to Jerrel about what she had been up to, so she tried to keep his attention on her.

"Baby, where your mom and dad go?"

"They bounced right after the ceremony, but they said they were so proud of you."

Kiara was tired of following them, but she wasn't gonna stop at nothing to let the world know just how sneaky Yaya was.

"Jerrel, Jerrel, you better watch your girl, she sneaky as hell!" Kiara called out.

Jerrel opened the door for Yaya then walked around to the driver side. As he got in, he looked over towards Yaya.

"Man, what the fuck that bitch talking about, I thought y'all were friends? Ain't she the same one that helped get you that job?"

"We were until I told her that we were in a serious relationship. She's been acting crazy since then. She yelling out you need to watch me and I be up under you all day."

Jerrel drove off laughing at Kiara. "That bitch got some fucking issues. Before we met, she did try to fuck, but I wasn't feeling her ass. I knew I wanted you since day one."

Yaya joined him in laughter. "That girl is a loser."

~

After having a celebration dinner, Jerrel took Yaya back to his place. They hadn't been there in a few days, but since he was taking her on a vacation for her graduation, he wanted her to pack up some stuff.

"I gotta go run a few errands and tie up some loose ends, but in a few hours, I'll be all yours, baby."

"Do you really have to leave me, baby? What if Jacques comes here on that bullshit?"

"Man, he not gon' be on no bullshit. I'll be back in a few hours. I gotta get this last shit together, then we'll be leaving first thing in the morning," he said, giving her a kiss.

Yaya laid across the bed pretending to be upset, but she was secretly waiting for him to walk out the door. Soon as Jerrel was long gone from the house, Yaya put her plan in motion. Pulling out her phone, she called

Kiara, praying that she had the same number from the phone that she had stolen.

"What the fuck are you calling me for?"

"Damn, Kiara, I thought that we were friends. You really trying to fuck shit up with me and Jerrel when you pretended to be so happy for us."

Kiara held the phone not saying shit. She wanted to see the bitch in person so she could beat her ass. She knew that Yaya wasn't a real fighter and could easily be tossed around.

"Why don't you pull up so we can talk?" Kiara suggested.

Yaya had already put some pants on and was lacing up her gym shoes. She had promised herself that she was done killing muthafuckas, but Kiara was gonna be a pain in her ass and fuck shit up for her. Yaya caught an Uber to the neighborhood park, so that her and Kiara could meet up. She really wanted to convince Kiara that she didn't have shit to do with these low life's death, but if she started to act crazy and not listen, Yaya was ready to silence her.

Arriving fifteen minutes early, she sat on the park bench waiting. She constantly looked around to watch out for Kiara. The last thing she wanted was for her to try to sneak her.

"What's up, Yaya?"

Yaya turned around to find Kiara walking up.

"Hey."

"I find it funny that now you wanna talk when earlier, you didn't have shit to say in front of your boyfriend."

Yaya stood up. "Kiara, I really didn't know what you were trying to pull, but I didn't want no part in your loud outburst," she said, playing it cool.

"I'm not gonna play no games with you, girl. I have a feeling that you're responsible for the death of two people."

Yaya laughed. "You must be smoking dope 'cause you talking crazy as fuck right now."

"I'm not on shit, bitch. I just found it crazy how we just so happened to fall out and then boom, my fucking phone went missing. See, what you didn't know was that James had come over to the house that night when someone pretended to be me on my phone texting him. I knew from jump that it was you. It wasn't until the next day when they found him butt naked and dead with his dick cut off that I knew you did that."

Yaya cut her off. "Bitch, you really are crazy. How do you think I was able to do all that to a grown as man?" She said, trying not to show her poker face.

"That all got me thinking about Rod. You said that you heard him leave that night, but his baby mama said he never showed up that night. Nobody was in that house but me and you. Why would you kill my cousin?"

By now, Kiara was angry and fighting her tears.

"Listen, Kiara, I really don't know what you're talking about," Yaya lied.

Kiara didn't respond with words. Instead, she quickly swung on Yaya, hitting her in the lip, causing it to leak.

"Bitch!" Yaya yelled, swinging back.

Yaya had never been a fighter, but she had years of anger built up in her and now, she was finally about to let it out. The girls fought each other as if they never were friends. Although she tried, Yaya wasn't winning that fight at all. Kiara was getting the best of her. For a minute, Yaya prayed that someone was watching and would soon break it up. That was until Yaya finally pulled out her mace and sprayed Kiara in the eyes.

"Stupid bitch!" Kiara yelled out, grabbing her face.

Yaya got up from the ground, now happy that no one was watching them and the park was empty dark.

"Yeah, bitch, you were right. I killed both of them stupid, pussy hungry muthafuckas. Rod ate my pussy so good before I killed him, and then I poured that bleach down his throat to wash away my pussy juices. But James was just dumb. If he knew you weren't texting him because he was with you, why the fuck would he still go to the park? He really thought it was a chance that he could still hit?"

While Yaya took a pause, Kiara tried to attack her again, but sadly ran straight into the blade that Yaya was holding. Kiara tried to let out a loud scream. Afraid that someone might hear her, Yaya gave her a stab to the throat. Kiara's body hit the ground as she tried to fight for her life.

"I really liked you, Kiara, and considered you as a friend until you started getting in my business. I never told you this, but when I was younger, Jackson had James and Rod kill my brother then my mama as she begged for my brother not to leave us. I was just trying to get revenge, that's it. I'm sorry you couldn't keep your nose out of my business. We could have still been friends, dummy."

Yaya slowly walked away, leaving Kiara to breathe her final breath.

~

"Where you been?"

Standing there dressed in all black and with her hoodie on, tied tight around her head, Yaya stopped in her tracks. Jacques had just caught her coming into the house after killing Kiara.

"I'm not your woman, and I'm for damn sure not fucking you!" She snapped back.

"You weird as hell. I don't see why my brother fuck with your ass so heavy."

Yaya shook her head as she prayed he wasn't about to get on her nerves.

"Look, boy, you really need to stay out of our business. I make your brother happy and that's all that matters, right?" She argued.

Jacques chuckled. "He just pussy whooped for the moment, but once I tell him the truth, he will get rid of your ass."

Yaya started pacing the floor, wondering what the fuck he was talking about. "What the fuck are you talking about?"

"My auntie fucked up and my sister's dead. Do you know what they had in common?"

"No, but I'm pretty sure you about to try to put something together."

"I replayed that night over and over in my head. Then it hit me that I saw you talking to Aunt Janet right before her and Jewel were rushed to the hospital. The doctors are talking about alcohol poison, and I'm starting to believe that you had something to do with it."

"Oh, ok. So I'm the weird one when you're trying to accuse me of doing harm to someone. You're so jealous of me and Jerrel's happiness that you would go this far, Jacques? What's the real problem? Are you mad 'cause your brother got me first?" She questioned.

Jacques chuckled. "I never wanted you, bitch."

"Bitch, bitch!" Yaya screamed as she started to hit Jacques.

He was raised to never hit a woman, so he grabbed her arms, trying to get her to calm down. "See, I told everybody your ass was crazy."

Yaya kept trying to fight Jacques and refused to stop. "You will not fuck up my happiness with Jerrel!" She continued to scream.

Jacques was tired of trying to hold her down but refused to knock her crazy ass out. Instead, he slammed her down on the couch before backing up.

"You crazy as hell, and I will be talking to my bro in the morning before he leaves."

Yaya watched as Jacques walked out the door. She wanted to chase him down and hurt him, but she wasn't sure how she was gonna explain everything to Jerrel. Jacques got in his car, not really knowing his next move, but he for sure didn't wanna be in the house with Yaya's crazy ass.

Thinking over their conversation, she was right about him being jealous that Jerrel got her first. Him and his brother used to fuck hoes and then pass them with no problem, but Jerrel had become a bitch and fell in love. Jacques got out of the car then walked back into the house. He wanted to apologize to Yaya. Truthfully, he had been giving her a hard time because of jealousy. As he got to Jerrel's room, he knocked on the door. Yaya had just got a text saying that he had just pulled up.

"Come in."

Jacques walked in. "Look, I'm sorry about everything."

"Leave me alone, Jacques, and get away from me!" She yelled, knowing Jerrel was there.

Yaya stood up to get closer to him.

"I said I was sorry, crazy ass!" He yelled, grabbing her.

"Please, Jacques, let me go and leave me alone!" She yelled.

Jerrel ran into the room to see Jacques holding Yaya by the arms and her face full of tears with a busted lip and swollen jaw. Not knowing the whole story, Jerrel started attacking Jacques.

"You hit my girl, nigga?" He yelled, giving his brother a quick three-piece combo.

Jacques didn't wanna fight his bro, but he refused to stand there and just accept the ass whooping.

"Ok, Jerrel, that's enough!" Yaya screamed, playing her role.

After five more minutes, she finally pulled Jerrel off his brother.

"Man, fuck you and that crazy bitch!" He yelled, walking out the room.

Jerrel tried to go after him, but Yaya stopped him. "Baby, chill out, he had enough."

"Fuck that, look at your fucking face, baby."

Yaya started giving Jerrel sweet kisses trying to calm him down. "I'm ok, baby. Let's get some rest so we can be on our way to Jamaica in the morning."

Jerrel wanted to fight again, but Yaya said what she said and had him wrapped up in her feelings.

As they laid in the bed, Jerrel's mind was racing.

"Yaya, what happened when I left?"

She had already thought her story out and was ready. "I had just put on some night cloths so I could pack some stuff before bed, and he busted in the door. He started talking shit and grabbing on me. I was scared and hit him. That's when he went crazy and started beating my ass. Once he was done, he left out. I grabbed my phone to call you, but he came back trying to apologize. That's when you came in to save me. Baby, I never saw him like that before, I was so scared."

Everything played out like a movie in Jerrel's head, so he believed everything that she said.

"I'm about to go fuck him up again. That bitch as nigga in there sleep and shit like everything's all good."

Yaya didn't want them to speak to one another. She was scared that Jacques was gonna tell what really happened.

"No, baby, stay here with me," she whined.

Seeing that he was still amped up, she slowly started kissing on his chest before making her way down to his dick. She knew exactly how to clear his mind

# Chapter 9

Jerrel was woken by his 5am alarm.

"Damn," he mumbled.

Not feeling Jerrel's body pressed against hers anymore, Yaya sat right up next to him.

"You ok, baby? Did you sleep ok?"

"Yeah, I'm good although my body a little sore."

"Do you want a massage?"

"Nah, we really need to be getting ready to go."

After a long shower together and a fuck session, the couple was all smiles getting ready for their trip.

"Baby, I can't wait to be in that water and laid under that sun."

"You're gonna love it, I promise you that," Jerrel assured her.

Minutes later, Jerrel was loading the trunk with their bags. He hated how things went down with his brother. He was still pissed and didn't wanna say shit to him at the time but had planned on working everything out when him and Yaya came back.

As he sat in the truck waiting, he started to think that she was taking too long or that Jacques had probably did something to her. Walking into the house, Jerrel met up with Yaya walking out of the kitchen.

"Damn, baby, what's taking you do long? I know you ain't change your mind."

Yaya laughed. "I was grabbing a bottle of water and apple for the ride."

Jerrel gave Yaya a kiss. "Come on, baby, let's get out of here."

The couple drove off without a care in the world. For the next two weeks, Jamaica was gonna be there home. Fuck whatever was happening in Detroit.

Jacques woke up feeling like a complete ass. He had been fucking with Jerrel about Yaya and got his ass beat. He knew that they were gone, so he had time to clear his mind. Picking up the phone, Jacques called his dad to explain everything to him.

"Dad, I really need to talk to you about that crazy bitch that Jerrel be fucking with."

"Man, I don't wanna hear that shit. I told you to leave your brother and his girl alone!" Jackson yelled through the phone.

Jacques hated how no one would listen to him.

"Dad, would you just listen?"

"Look, I'll be over there in a minute."

Jackson got up so that he could go talk some sense into his son.

Soon as Jacques opened the door for his dad, they went into the front room to talk. Jackson watched as his son rolled up his blunt.

"What's up, Jacques? I didn't come over here to watch you smoke."

"Man, that bitch is crazy…" he started to explain.

Just as he lit his blunt…*BOOM!*

~

Jerrel and Yaya ran out of the water and collapsed on their beach towel.

"Baby, I've never had so much fun. I love you so much."

"I love your ass too, that's why I'm gonna make sure your summer is filled with memories."

They shared a kiss.

"Good 'cause I don't even wanna go back to Detroit no time soon. You were right about loving a nice get away."

"Hell yeah, baby. Then not having my phone was a fucking bonus. I don't wanna be bothered with all that bullshit back at home.'

Yaya couldn't do shit but smile. She had convinced Jerrel to leave his phone off while they were on vacation, so that they could enjoy their time together. The last thing she wanted was for him to get a call telling him how Jacques was blown up in a house explosion. Yaya got comfortable on her towel and soon had a flashback of her mother and brother's death. It was so clear as if she was still in the closet watching. Yaya had never told anyone the truth about what happened that day, but it never left her mind.

*"Come on, man, I found the bag. Let's get the fuck out of here!" James yelled.*

Yaya watched as they ran out the house. Crying hard, she climbed out of the closet.

*"Mommy, get up!" She yelled.*

*Yaya cried her eyes out knowing that her family was long gone.*

*She snapped. "How could y'all just leave me like that? I hate y'all! What am I supposed to do now?" She cried.*

*Not thinking completely, she decided that she didn't wanna live anymore without them. Yaya ran into the garage to get the gasoline for the lawnmower then poured it around the house. She was determined to go with her mom and brother. She laid next to Darron and her mom as the fire started to spread around the house. It wasn't until the flames finally hit the living room that she decided dying like that would be too much. Jumping up from the floor, Yaya hurried to run out the door. That's when she ran down the street to her mama's best friend house.*

Yaya jumped up from her sleep. "Jerrel."

"Yeah, baby, what's up?" Jerrel asked, holding her a little tighter.

"I love you so much."

"I love you too," he said, giving her a kiss.

# About the Author

Author T. Friday was born and raised in Detroit, Michigan. At the age of 35, she is the mother of five children. Three handsome boys ages 18, 13, and 12 and two beautiful girls ages 8 and 7.

At a very early age T. Friday became in love with reading books, such as Babysitters Club and Goosebumps books by R.L Stine. It wasn't until she was in her early teens when she was introduced to Urban Fiction books. That's when she knew that she wanted a career in the book industry. January of 2016 T. Friday had her left leg amputated and that was when she realized that she had been taking her life for granted. She decided to do something that she loved to do. She picked up a pen and some paper then started writing. In May of 2017 T. Friday signed her first contract with Racquel Williams who is the creator of RWP. Now in 2020 she is the author of 19 books. She has plans to continue writing until one day all of her books are turned into movies.

**T. Friday's Book Catalog**

Intrigued by a Savage's Love (Standalone)

Finding Love in a Real Boss 1

Finding Love in a Real Boss 2

Nasir & Kennedy: Luv in the Gutta (Standalone)

In Love with a Street Princess (Standalone)

To Be Loved by a Brick Boy 1

To Be Loved by a Brick Boy 2

To Be Loved by a Brick Boy 3

When Love Calls the Shots (Standalone)

All Cried Out: Loving a Detroit Nigga 1

All Cried Out: Loving a Detroit Nigga 2

Yearning for the Love of a Thug (Standalone)

Saving all my Love for a Young Boss 1

Saving all my Love for a Young Boss 2

Javarri and Jewel: His Love Wasn't Enough (Standalone)

Tears Shed from Loving a Trap Nigga 1

Tears Shed from Loving a Trap Nigga 2

A Detroit Nigga Finessed my Love (Standalone)

Pretty Bitches get Even (Standalone)

***ALL SERIES ARE COMPLETED***

# Author's Contact Information

 Author T Friday

 Authortfriday

 @FridayAuthor

If you haven't already sign up for my email blast for new updates on all my books Messiah.nf@gmail.com

**ALL MY BOOKS CAN BE FOUND ON AMAZON.COM** Read a book, leave a review on Amazon or Goodreads, and tell a friend.

www.ingramcontent.com/pod-product-compliance
Lightning Source LLC
Chambersburg PA
CBHW071249150726
48001CB00018B/475